MW01443833

SOUVENIRS

T. L. Bishop

Copyright © 2022 T. L. Bishop

All rights reserved. This book or any portion thereof may not be reproduced or used in any manner whatsoever without the express written permission of the author except for the use of brief quotations in a book review.

This is a work of fiction. Names, characters, businesses, places, events, and incidents are products of the author's imagination. Any resemblance to actual persons, living or dead, is purely coincidental.

ISBN: 9798794817942

1

The light was shining so beautifully through the stained-glass window by the fireplace. The star in the center allowed the light to filter through more brightly than normal. Gracie remembered that GiGi always loved stars. The rich coffee aroma filled the air throughout the house and Gracie hurried downstairs. She loved staying with her grandmother. Although Gracie was now in her twenties, she cherished the wisdom and love GiGi gave her when she was able to spend time with her.

Looking around the beach bungalow, Gracie saw remnants of a life lived well. Special wooden shorebirds from treasured family trips, paintings, a clay figurine sculpted by her great-grandmother, family pictures, a large portrait of Christ over the piano, and lots of baskets everywhere. The picture of Christ reminded Gracie of her mother's favorite scripture, Psalm 139. These things were all treasured souvenirs in GiGi's home that were special to Gracie. Many of the items belonged to Gracie's mother, Joy. As Gracie was admiring all the collectibles, she noticed GiGi nearby.

GiGi always seemed to float into a room. She was still attractive despite her years with eyes that sparkled and thick white hair supporting an ornate headband that she still wore from her teen years with sparkles and beading that looked brand new. "I am so glad you are here, Gracie," GiGi said. "I have a surprise for you before you go back to college. A souvenir, we'll call it."

"What?" Gracie was without words. She had come to GiGi's beach bungalow to get away for a much-needed break from college. She had been working and studying diligently and rarely had time to relax. She was also trying to heal from a very hurtful semi-breakup from her long-time boyfriend, Max.

"I have some things that I want you to have, especially since your mama is gone, but let's have our coffee first. Do you mind pulling your favorite cinnamon rolls out of the oven? I need you to get that bowl of icing on the counter and ice those rolls while they are warm. Thank you, Luv."

Gracie smiled and followed directions. Gracie loved being in the kitchen, working beside her grandmother. It made her feel as if she were with her mom whom she missed so. She thought back to a time when she was a little girl. She and Mama would escape to the beach to visit GiGi.

She remembered a time when they found a bucket full of sand dollars and starfish. That day happened to be her fourteenth birthday, when Mama gave Gracie a golden heart locket and bracelet. Originally, Mama had received them both on her fourteenth birthday from GiGi and Papa. They had spent the day at the beach and had a clambake that evening to celebrate. She recalled the fire, the laughter, the gifts, and the stars.

"Earth to Gracie! How are those rolls coming along?" GiGi asked with a sweet smile.

"Oh, I'm sorry. I was thinking about when Mama was here with us at the beach. I'll hurry because I am starving, and no one makes cinnamon rolls like you!" Gracie decorated the buns with such finesse, as if she were painting a masterpiece. She gazed out the kitchen window at the stormy, wind-tossed sea and realized that she felt the same way inside… turbulent, restless, and aching.

* * *

As GiGi poured coffee from her antique Blue Willow coffee pot, Gracie walked over to the counter to get the matching creamer and sugar containers. Gracie had always loved the quilted tablecloth that her great grandma, Sophie, had made. The tints of blues and yellows again reminded her of how she felt inside. Sunshine yellow to designate being with GiGi, and yet deep blue as the ocean as well. She missed her mama and Max so much, and she didn't think that time would change that.

"I love being here with you, GiGi," Gracie said. "It's just so peaceful, and I love Grandma Sophie's quilt."

"Gracie, you know that some people associate the colors in this quilt with *hope*, don't you?"

"No, I really didn't know that."

"Well, according to the internet, wink, wink: green equals willpower, yellow equals happiness, blue equals hope, red equals rage, orange equals avarice, indigo equals compassion, violet equals love, black equals death. Life is full of these colors, especially blue, indigo, and violet. Grandma Sophie used to tell me, 'It's a good life if you don't weaken'." She winked and said with a giggle, "But that's another story for another day. How is your coffee, Dear?"

Gracie replied, "Wonderful. Your coffee is best because you grind your own coffee beans. If you show me how to do it, I will make coffee in the morning for us." She noticed GiGi looking down for a moment.

"Is that okay, GiGi?"

"Yes, that would be wonderful." GiGi stood up and said, "I'll get us a napkin." As she stood up and turned around, Gracie noticed GiGi using her crisp white apron to wipe her eyes.

"What is it, GiGi?"

She turned back around and said, "You are such a dear. No one has made coffee for me since Papa has been gone. Such a sweet memory of Papa making coffee. It took him awhile to catch on, but when he did, his coffee was the best. What would you like to do today, Gracie?"

"The beach is always my first choice, but you already know that."

"Okay, then, why don't you take a morning walk on the beach and then we'll take a drive into town to run some errands so I can show you off? Hopefully, we will be back in time for you to take a sunset walk along the beach after dinner. How does that sound?"

"Sounds great, GiGi. I'll finish the dishes if you want to get your list for the market ready?"

"I like the way you think, young 'un!"

Gracie began washing the morning dishes and gazed out the kitchen window again. The sea seemed to be calming some. The red beach warning flag was changed to yellow. Gracie remembered that the beach flag signage was important to follow:

GREEN: LOW HAZARD – Calm Condition, Exercise Caution
YELLOW: MEDIUM HAZARD – Moderate Surf and/or Moderate Currents
RED: HIGH HAZARD – High Surf and/or Strong Currents
DOUBLE RED: WATER CLOSED TO PUBLIC
PURPLE: Marine Pests Present

Her thoughts wandered back to her last day at school when she received the phone call from Max.

"I won't be coming with you to the beach for spring break, because I have other plans." The silence had been deafening. Gracie remembered sitting in silence as his words seemed to stab at her heart. "I have an opportunity to do my internship in Europe."

Gracie's mind raced.

"Gracie, are you there?"

She bit her lip and wiped the tears, then responded, "Why did you wait until the day before we are leaving to tell me? Something about this doesn't quite seem right. What *aren't* you telling me, Max?"

"We can talk about this when I get back," he said.

"No, let's finish this conversation now."

"Okay, if that's how you want it, here you go. I may have an opportunity for a full-time position after the internship is over. I will return to Europe after graduation if a job is extended to me. Hey, maybe you can come for a visit?"

"I knew there was something going on."

"Why would you say that?"

"Come on, Max, I have known you, loved you, and grown up with you, and I know what this means."

"What are you saying?" Max inquired.

"What are *you* saying, Max?" Gracie countered.

"I am trying to say goodbye."

2

"Hey, GiGi, if you have your list ready, I think I'll wait until evening to take that walk on the beach."

"Okay, I'm ready if you are. Let's go. Shall we take the convertible or the truck? You are the chauffeur, so it's your choice," she asked as she headed toward the door.

"Probably should take the truck. We might have lots to buy today," Gracie said with a huge, little girl grin.

The '57 Chevy truck was spotless as always and ready to go. It was Papa's baby, and he treated it that way. He would have been proud to see Gracie driving a standard pickup now. It took several trips up and down the coast to finally get it.

The drive up to Seashore Lane was always so enjoyable to Gracie. She loved watching the seagulls and pelicans on the beach as they drove. The warm salty breezes were so inviting.

"Well, here, we are," GiGi said. "I need to drop off some things at the Post Office. If you would like to look around, I will meet you at the Seaside Market in about 30 minutes."

"Okay, see you in a few," Gracie replied. "I am

heading to the seaside shops until then."

Gracie watched as GiGi walked away. The straw hat covering that beautiful white hair and sixty's movie star sunglasses secluding those beautiful blue eyes gave the impression that she might be a movie star incognito. GiGi's pale faded jeans and Papa's work-shirt tied up made her seem so much younger than her years. Such a beautiful soul, Gracie thought.

The seaside village seemed to be the same as when Gracie last visited. She loved the open concept of the restaurants, coffee shops, and all the little shops around the square. The bookstore was having a sale, so Gracie hurried in to make a purchase for her time at the beach later. Gracie found an old copy of one of her favorite novels and bought it quickly, remembering it was one of Mama's favorite movies.

"There you are," GiGi said, as they entered the seaside market.

"The market hasn't changed a bit, has it?"

"No, not really," Gracie said as she gazed up and down the walls and aisles.

Gracie loved the fact that you could buy the best home-made pastries, along with a great cup of java. You could complete your visit by sitting out on their porch reading the most current city newspaper and visiting with the locals. The displays inside were perfect; fresh fruits and vegetables, seafood and steak, canned foods, and condiments lining the walls all the way to the ceiling.

GiGi noticed a few items on the top shelves that they needed for tonight's feast. "I will have to get some help to get those."

"I think I can climb the ladder to get it for you, GiGi."

"No, they like to get it for you, especially when you are old like me," she laughed.

Gracie noticed Sam the owner and thought to herself that he hasn't changed in many years.

"Good morning, Sam! Would you be able to get a few items for me from the top shelf?" GiGi asked.

Sam replied, "I haven't seen you in a few days. I hope that you are doing well?"

"Yes, I am doing fine. My granddaughter is here for a visit, so I have been getting things ready the last few days."

"Beau, would you mind helping Ms. Douglas out with a few items?" Sam asked.

"I'd be glad to," he answered in a soft but firm voice.

Gracie continued her search for goodies for the beach, not noticing the young man assisting GiGi. "I have some things to add now, but I will pay for them," Gracie said as she backed her way over to the magazine rack.

"A girl's gotta eat, too. Don't forget some snacks!" Beau said as he carried GiGi's grocery items to the register. The sound of his voice made Gracie swirl around quickly to respond. She opened her mouth to speak, but nothing came out.

"Cat got your tongue?" Beau asked.

Gracie could feel her face lighting up like the 4th of July.

"This is my granddaughter who has come for a visit, Beau. You can stop by some evening to say hello and show Gracie around if you like?" GiGi asked. "Who knows, maybe she'll come back to see us later this summer."

"Who knows?" Beau teased. "Maybe she *will* come back for another visit this summer!"

Still reeling from the first comment, Gracie shuffled over to pay for her items. "I'd better run by the bookstore, so I have another enchanting book for the beach. I will meet you back at the car."

The screen door slammed a little harder than Gracie intended and as she was walking out, she heard GiGi say, "Gracie has always been a little shy."

The ride home was quiet. GiGi didn't even seem to notice how uncomfortable she was by GiGi inviting Beau to stop by.

Once home, Gracie hurried inside with the groceries to help GiGi put them away. "Looks like we will have 'Sophie's Special' for dinner if that is okay with you?"

Gracie replied, "That would be splendid. I haven't had that since… you know…"

"I know, Dear."

Sophie's Special was something that Mama had created for her grandma. She named it after her because Grandma Sophie loved bacon and cheese.

<u>SOPHIE'S SPECIAL</u>
Layer the following ingredients to form a sandwich:
One piece of toast

Lettuce
Ripe tomato slices
Onion (optional)
Two boiled eggs sliced
Four pieces crisp bacon
One piece of toast
After layering, cut the sandwich in half and drizzle melted Velveeta cheese of the top.

"GiGi, it was Mama's creation, so who cares about calories?"

"Atta girl, Gracie! Let's take our plates out to eat on the porch. I have some freshly brewed iced tea with lemon slices out there waiting on us."

Sophie's Special tasted so much better than Gracie had remembered. "This is so good, GiGi, but I think I have it all over me."

"I do, too. Gracie. After you're finished, why don't you run along down to the beach, and we'll have our dessert when you get back?"

"Okay, that sounds good."

As they were finishing their dinner, several bicyclers rode by and waved. One of the riders called out, "Hey Gracie, if you'd like to borrow a bicycle, our bicycle club rides every evening at this time. We will pick you up on our way! Hope to see you tomorrow!"

It was Beau. She could see his blue topaz eyes a long way from where Gracie was standing.

"Well, he certainly has some blue eyes, doesn't he?" GiGi chuckled.

"Yes, they are hard to miss," Gracie responded.

As she headed down toward the beach, she said to herself, "Almost like a neon sign."

"I have known Beau for years as he grew up here," GiGi called to Gracie.

The sun was beginning to set along the beach, and the spectrum of colors were lighting up the sky so magnificently with shades of pink, orange, and purple. GiGi's porch was perfect to watch the sunsets, but Gracie loved feeling the wind in her hair, and the cool water splashing up on her feet.

After walking down the beach, Gracie decided to sit down and enjoy the view. The sand was like powdered sugar and felt so good and warm against her body as she lay on the beach trying to read her book.

She kept thinking of Max and tried to block out every thought of him, his scent, his smile, his green eyes. Why didn't he share with her about his internship? Why did he wait until the last minute to choose to not come with her? Gracie could feel the tears rising and flowing down her cheeks like the waves. She didn't understand and refused to let thoughts of Max ruin her time here at the sea wondering why. *"One door closes and another opens,"* she thought. *"Just be sure that the door doesn't hit you in the —! Oops, here comes the rain."*

Gracie grabbed her book and ran up to the awning of one of the beach cafes. A cup of coffee sounded good. She thought she might start reading her book outside at the tables there. She began reading and noticed the bicyclers riding up the street. All were soaked to the skin.

"Gracie, are you buying tonight?"

Oh no, she thought to herself. "Sure, what would you like?"

"I'll have the same as you. Are you having a mocha latte or regular coffee with cream?"

"The latter. Short ride tonight?" she teased.

Beau smiled, and Gracie noticed that Beau seemed a little embarrassed. Could he be a little shy, too, she wondered? He wasn't the tough guy that she thought he might be and that was good. It was incredibly good. She had her fill of the tough guys.

"How long are you here, Gracie?"

"I'm here until Saturday."

"Would you like to go down to the pier with me and some friends Friday night? We are going to have a clam bake, then ride the amusement rides and hang out at the pier. They usually have a local band playing there, too on Friday nights. Do you dance?"

"I haven't danced in a while, but it sounds like fun. I will check with GiGi to make sure she doesn't have anything planned for us. I can let you know tomorrow if that is okay? It will be my last night here, so I hate to leave her by herself."

"I am sure the week is going to fly for you. You can let me know tomorrow if you want to join our bicycle group. Thanks for the coffee, Gracie. Enjoy your book."

"Okay, thanks, Beau. See you tomorrow."

"See you later." His blue eyes sparkled.

Beau rode off, and Gracie watched him until she couldn't see him any longer. He seemed to ride away in the direction of GiGi's house. The thought of his white, straight teeth and tanned body complimented by his sun kissed and tousled brown hair made Gracie drift away even further. He was even more attractive than she remembered.

Something inside her was allowing her to have hope. Hope that GiGi didn't have anything planned for them on Friday night.

Once Beau disappeared into the shadows, Gracie decided that she should head back home before the next cloud burst. It was such a beautiful walk home.

When she arrived, GiGi had left her a note on the kitchen table that read:

"Gracie,
I need to run over to check on a neighbor. Be back soon. Max called and left a different number for you to call or text when you return. He said you aren't answering any messages or emails. He said if you could not call tonight, he would try again Friday night to catch you.
Love, GiGi
P.S. Dessert is on the buffet."

Gracie sighed and walked over to the buffet to pick up her dessert. As she passed by the kitchen to get her fresh strawberry pie, she re-read the note. She thought about Max for a moment, then threw the note in the wastebasket. How many times had she received a note like that? Too many to count.

3

The morning light woke Gracie as she lay across the high-back antique bed. Gracie thought about all that they had done so far because the week was flying by. Here it was already Wednesday. Today was 'work in the garden' day.

Gracie loved helping GiGi in her garden. She told Gracie that the key to a beautiful garden is to add a foot or so to the border every year because it takes a lifetime to have the garden of your dreams.

Gracie remembered 'the secret garden' that she and Mama had together when she was a small child. They would dress up and have tea parties there. GiGi still has some of the plants along with the tiny wrought iron table and chairs that they used. She remembered the funny hats and high heels that they wore. So many sweet memories of Mama always flood her mind when she visited GiGi's.

This week Gracie and GiGi were going to add a bunny bench and small water pond filled with ornamental plants and koi to her garden. Everything was to be delivered early to get the job done.

"Breakfast is ready. Rise and shine."

Gracie could smell the bacon cooking. "I'll be right there."

GiGi said, "I see your note in the wastebasket. I'm guessing that you saw the telephone number?"

"Yes, I saw it, but I'm not calling," Gracie said looking down at her plate then out the window.

"I see," said GiGi with a surprised look on her face. "Have some nourishment, Dear."

Breakfast was quick and the morning seemed to fly by, working in the garden. She and GiGi were an effective team. GiGi was in charge and Gracie was her helper, just like in the old days.

"Beau said he would bring the koi over later when he delivered the other supplies this morning."

"Beau will be bringing the fish here, too?" Gracie asked with a slight smile and twinkle in her eye.

"Yes, he is always doing something for me. He's an extremely sweet young man. And those blue eyes…"

"I am finding that out, GiGi. He is taking me out with his friends Friday night before I head back if that is okay with you?"

GiGi had her back to Gracie and said, "That will be quite fine, Dear."

Gracie could not see the huge smile on GiGi's face as she finished planting the last flower.

"Since we have worked so hard this morning and gotten so much done, what do you say I treat you to a girls' day with a mani-pedi this afternoon?"

Gracie was surprised, but added, "Only if you get one too, GiGi."

"I have never had one." GiGi made a funny face to make Gracie laugh.

"All the more reason for you to go with me. I will

buy lunch for us at the Seaside Tea Room, okay?"

"What about Beau dropping the fish off?" Gracie asked.

"He won't be coming until after 6, so we'd better get ready to go." GiGi hurried along and added, "Can you be ready in 30 minutes?"

"I sure can."

Gracie hurried off to get her shower. She thought about her mama as she began to get ready. Mama would have loved going with her and GiGi for a girl's day out together. She was always the life of the party.

Gracie loved walking the sea path to town, but GiGi liked to drive the convertible on fun trips.

"Meet you in the car, Gracie!"

"Okay, almost ready!"

Gracie opened the vanity drawer to get a brush and noticed a postcard under the liner of the drawer. The postcard had the picture of a Ferris wheel on the front near the sea. As she read the front, it was from GiGi's little seaside town and looked old. She turned it over and noticed beautiful hand-written calligraphy that read:

"Up high on a Ferris wheel at the edge of the sea,
Starry, starry skies and moonlight, your arms wrapped around me."

She looked at it again and noticed two people at the top of the Ferris wheel, snuggled close together, gazing at the moon and stars.

Beep, beep. GiGi honked her horn, so Gracie

grabbed the brush, slid the postcard into her purse and ran out to the car.

* * *

Town seemed busy today as GiGi pulled into her favorite shady parking spot under the pier.

"I think I just may have dessert for lunch today," Gracie said.

"The key lime pie here is to die for. You'd better wait to see the revised lunch menu and have both." GiGi let out a belly laugh that Gracie hadn't heard in a while. GiGi had the best laugh. "We'll go light on dinner then." GiGi winked.

"Well, if you say so," Gracie agreed.

As Gracie was opening the door for GiGi, she heard a familiar and sweet voice behind her. "Well, hello, Gracie."

"Working today, Beau?" she asked.

"Yes, just making deliveries up the street. You girls in for the day or just for lunch?"

"Lunch. Well, we are really here for dessert." GiGi let out another belly laugh, and it made Gracie and Beau laugh even harder.

"See you tonight, Beau."

"You can count on it, Gracie."

Beau smiled that heart-breaker smile of his, and Gracie and GiGi both seemed to melt for a moment. He turned and hurried off to finish his deliveries.

GiGi grabbed her heart. "Whew!"

Gracie just smiled, but she knew exactly what GiGi meant.

* * *

After lunch and pedis, the girls decided to stop in at the Seaside Surf Shop. "Do you have anything to wear to the clam bake Friday night, Dear?" GiGi asked.

"I didn't pack much since I was in such a hurry to get here. I sure didn't plan on having any social activities either." Gracie leaned in to look in the store window.

"I see a great bikini and cover up that would fit you perfectly," GiGi said.

Grimacing, Gracie said, "I was thinking more along the lines of shorts and a new t-shirt."

"I really didn't think you would go for it. Just having a little fun with you, girlie."

"There it is. What do you think, GiGi?"

"Well, hurry up and try it on."

The hour seemed to fly by, and Gracie did find a few new things. It had been a while since she had gotten to buy anything new. GiGi loved to spoil her, and Gracie loved her for that.

"How about a pair of matching flip-flops?"

"I won't need anything new for the beach for my feet."

GiGi made a funny face to make Gracie laugh aloud.

"If you have all that you need, Dear, I'll get these paid for. We will have a little more work tonight after we receive our deliveries."

Gracie thought to herself, *"If I had all that I need...* Max's last words kept haunting her and she felt a tiny tear slide down her cheek. *"If I had all that I need... No, I*

23

sure don't."

"The fish are coming!"

"I almost forgot. I will hurry, GiGi."

* * *

As they pulled into the drive, someone had parked along the street and was around back unloading the fish.

Gracie hurriedly hopped out of the car and to her surprise, it wasn't Beau. Disappointment was written all over her face. She turned around to go in to change her clothes to get back to work.

Looking down as she walked toward the back yard, she almost ran into the arbor.

"Gotcha!" It was Beau. He pulled her back around into the arbor and held her for a moment. "Are you okay? You look a little woozy."

Woozy, she thought. If he only knew how weak in the knees she really was at that moment. "I'm fine. You just startled me, that's all."

"Oh, okay. See you back at the koi pond. I'll show you how to finish the last part so you can join the bicycle club tonight if you're still interested in coming along with the group?"

"Sure! I still would love to come along."

"I have the perfect bike for you, so you won't even have to rent one."

"I have GiGi's bike if you don't mind me riding with a basket on mine?" She winked.

"Either way, let's get the job finished. It's almost time." Beau glanced at his watch.

"A watch and no phone?" Gracie asked.

"Yes, I try to keep my summers simple and uncomplicated. Phone is in the truck, though, just in case!" He smiled that killer smile.

"Just in case... what?"

"Just in case my boss needs me... or just in case you decide to call me."

Gracie blushed. "Well, I just might one of these days."

Beau smiled. "We'll ride by to pick you up, so get that bike ready and I'll— I mean, we'll see you in about an hour."

Gracie stood on the porch and watched Beau drive away. *"Wow, what just happened,"* she thought to herself. "Whew!" She sat down on the wicker rocking chair and looked out at the sea. The water was still a bit choppy, and the tide was beginning to come in. The seagulls were swirling above her, and she remembered an old song that played at her mama's funeral. "Seagull, you fly... across the horizon into the misty morning sun..." Gracie so longed to see her mama one more time. It seemed so very long ago that she was here. It was so peculiar to Gracie that her mother loved the era that her grandmother, GiGi, was born in, the bands, the styles, all of it.

"Low tide tonight," GiGi called and startled Gracie. "Maybe we'll find some good shells for you to take back with you to school, Gracie," GiGi said. "You still heading out with the bicycle group?"

"Yes, I won't be gone long."

"That is fine. It will give me a chance to complete a few things here, Dear."

Gracie headed in to start getting ready for the ride. The phone rang and GiGi answered it.

"Max, is that you? Our connection isn't clear. I can hardly hear you. No, Gracie isn't available right now. Would you like to leave a message? Yes… Okay, I will give her the message."

Gracie went on upstairs to the bedroom and started her bath. She did not want to hear what GiGi had to tell her. *"I'm going to need lots of bubbles tonight,"* she thought to herself and poured in four capfuls of bubble bath into the water.

As Gracie sank down into the bubbles, she heard a knock at the door. "Gracie, Max just called and left his new number again. He said to call him any time, but he needed to talk to you today or tomorrow."

"Okay, thank you, GiGi." *"Sorry, but this line has been disconnected,"* she thought to herself. She had no intentions of calling or messaging him back, not after everything that had happened.

Gracie hurried to get ready to meet the group and Beau.

"I see them coming down the road. It looks like there are about a dozen in the group! My bike is out front, and all cleaned up for you. I even put a bottle of water in your basket," GiGi said. "Maybe I should have gotten two bottles," she said with a sweet smile.

"Thank you, GiGi. I think one is okay for now. I will see you soon."

"I will leave the light on for you, Dear. Have an exciting time tonight."

"I hope to," Gracie said as she rode out to meet

the group.

"Let's go!"

"Race you all to the beach," Beau said as he hurried down the beach road with the others trying to cut around to beat him there.

"This is going to be a fun night," Gracie thought as she hurried to catch up.

The group rode about two miles down a quiet beach road. Riding on the sandy road was a little more difficult but good for burning calories. In the distance, a small fire was burning, and Gracie could hear more voices as they came closer. The sunset on the beach was unbelievable with all the vivid summer colors of orange, pink, blue, purple, and gold. The sunbeams were reflecting on the water, and it was breath-taking. Gracie jumped off her bike and just stared at the view for a moment.

"Amazing, isn't it?" Beau asked.

"I've never seen anything like it," Gracie said.

With his back to the sun, Beau looked at Gracie and said, "Neither have I."

Gracie looked up and Beau was standing remarkably close and was looking right in her eyes. They stood there without saying anything more for a moment, then Beau took Gracie's hand and said, "They're all waiting to meet you, so we'd better get over there."

Gracie smiled and said, "Okay."

"I want you all to meet my friend, Gracie! Gracie, this is the wild bunch." Beau proceeded to introduce everyone as they came over to say hello. The girls all hugged Gracie and told her that they hoped that she would be joining them again Friday night for the clam bake and fun at the pier. Gracie confirmed that she would be there and that would be her last night at the beach.

"We are the welcome wagon here and hope you come back this summer. We all get part-time jobs and spend the rest of the time at the beach or riding our bikes," said Vivian. "Not a bad way to spend your time!"

One of the guys added, "Some of us even take a few on-line classes," and made a funny face.

"Some of us don't because we work hard during the school year," one of the girls touted back.

In unison, the group said, "Here we go," as everyone burst out in laughter.

* * *

The night seemed to fly by. Gracie savored every moment with these sweet people. They all were kind and caring. She felt so blessed to be a part of this group.

"I think I might just have to nickname you Twinkle," Beau said as he reached for Gracie's hand. "Want to take a walk along the beach before we head back?"

"Sure. Maybe we'll find some shells since the tide is going back out now."

They walked and searched for shells. Everyone was out with their buckets, nets, and flashlights trying to see who could find the biggest shell. Baby crabs were running all along the beach, and it was a fun sight to see. Seagulls and sandpipers were all in on the fun.

Beau stopped and said, "Gracie, do you see those dolphins?"

"Where?"

Beau came up behind Gracie and turned her body toward the dolphins. He was so close that Gracie could feel the warmth of his body and smell his cool breeze scent, then as he pointed in the direction of the dolphins, he brushed her cheek.

"I don't see them."

"See, over there."

"No, I'm sorry, I don't see them."

"Keep watching and they will come up for air again... right about... There they are!" Beau pulled Gracie over to him and turned her head gently in their direction.

"I see them, I see them!" Gracie jumped and whirled around, and Beau was looking down at her again. Their eyes locked.

"Do you know why I am calling you Twinkle?"

"No, why?"

"Because your eyes always seem to twinkle when you look at me."

Gracie felt her face flush, and she was glad that it was getting dark outside.

"No one has ever told me that and I think I like it," Gracie said.

"Maybe they only twinkle when you look at me?"

"Maybe..."

Beau smiled and said, "I think we'd better get you back home before GiGi gets worried."

"Okay," Gracie said, but she didn't want the

moment to end. Beau brushed her cheek again, but this time with a soft, sweet, and quick kiss. Gracie felt that tug at her heart again. What just happened? she thought to herself.

"Wait for us!" They both laughed and yelled as they ran to catch up to the group as they were starting to pedal back to town.

As they entered the town square, the courthouse clock chimes were going off. It was midnight.

"We'll see you Friday night, Gracie!" the group said in unison.

"Okay, see you all later."

Beau stopped his bike and turned around to catch one more glimpse of Gracie as she walked into the house.

"What just happened?" he thought.

* * *

As Gracie walked up to the porch, GiGi was sitting in the rocking chair waiting for her with a fresh glass of iced, sweet tea. "How was your evening, Dear?"

"It was wonderful, GiGi."

"Have you thought much more about coming back for the summer?"

"I had planned to go to summer school, but I think I might take some on-line classes and bug you all summer if you don't mind?"

"Mind?" GiGi asked. "I am making plans for us already!" she said with that sparkle in her eye. She then let out another belly laugh, the kind that always made Gracie laugh. "I can't wait!"

"Good, then. I'll go ahead and give you one of

your gifts tonight instead of waiting until tomorrow night when you get home."

"Really? What is it, GiGi?"

"Let's call it a souvenir. I have a ring that belonged to your mama a long time ago, before she met your dad. She asked me to give it to you when the time was right, and I believe that time is now. Come inside, Dear."

GiGi walked over to her antique dresser and pulled out a little box. Inside was a small picture wrapped up with a ring.

"Open it, Dear."

Gracie opened the box and saw a picture of her mama with someone that she didn't recognize. "Who is that with Mama?" Gracie asked.

"It is Beau's father."

"What?" Gracie questioned. "I found an old postcard. I will show it to you." Gracie hurried to get her purse and pulled it out to show GiGi.

"Is this postcard from that time?"

"Yes, it is, Dear."

"Was this from Mama?"

"Yes, it was a postcard that she never did send."

"I am beginning to see now. I'm not related to Beau, am I?"

GiGi burst out in laughter. "No, Dear. Far from it."

"Thank goodness!" Gracie exclaimed.

They both started laughing, and Gracie couldn't help but wonder about this beautiful ring and the story behind the postcard.

Gracie didn't know, but GiGi had one more gift for her before she left tomorrow. GiGi had kept a message in a bottle from Mama that was still in the original bottle- cork, and all.

"We can talk more in the morning, but you'd better head off to bed now. We have a busy day tomorrow getting you ready to get back to school and then your night out with the bicycle club." GiGi winked and smiled as she left the room.

Gracie just couldn't imagine what this was all about and thought about GiGi's sweet smile and the way she smelled.

Gracie kissed GiGi and headed to bed. It was getting late. 11:00 p.m. here and who knows what time it was in Europe. Just then, the phone rang.

4

Gracie awoke remembering the late phone conversation last night. She did not have any tears left for what once was.

She then began thinking about the time with GiGi and how it always seemed to pass so quickly. Gracie did not want it to end. She could smell the coffee brewing and walked out to see GiGi busy in the kitchen preparing what seemed like a feast.

"GiGi, why didn't you call me to help you with all this?"

"I wanted to surprise you with your favorite brunch menu," GiGi replied.

"It looks like enough for an army."

"Well, maybe we should call in the troops and bicycle club."

"Oh, GiGi, really?"

"They are on their way! You'd better get dressed! It's your going-away brunch."

"Oh, GiGi, why do you spoil me so?"

"Because I can," GiGi replied and let out another one of her famous belly laughs. They both stood there laughing and giggling.

"We are eating in the Secret Garden, so you may notice that there are a few more chairs. We will begin carrying the food out when they start arriving. Now hurry up and get ready."

Gracie hurried to get ready before they all arrived.

"We all wanted your last days here to be special," GiGi hollered and then whispered to herself, "so you'll be sure to come back."

"GiGi, you already know I am coming back."

"You heard me? Yes, I know, Dear, but there are others that aren't quite so sure." She smiled and turned around to finish preparing the food.

Gracie proceeded back to her room to follow orders and smiled as she started to get ready for company. She pulled out her favorite "1977 E. Tour" t-shirt that was still hanging in Mama's closet, along with cut off blue jean shorts that also belonged to Mama. Wow, these are short, Mama, she thought as she pulled them on. She didn't realize that she and Mama were the same size at the same age.

As she worked along-side GiGi in the kitchen and garden, she felt such a bond that it made her tearful when she thought about going back to finish the semester at school. The sun shined so brightly, and the time passed quickly.

Gracie thought about the beautiful ring that GiGi had given her and wondered what the story was behind it. A star, a postcard, and a message in a bottle. So much to think about. More mysteries of Mama, she thought.

Guests started arriving early. "Here they come!" GiGi exclaimed and scurried off to the kitchen. "Gracie, come, Luv and help me get this food out on the tables."

Bicycles lined up on the sidewalk out front and

guests started filing inside in all directions. "We're here!" hollered the group.

Everyone had brought gifts and laid them on the table.

"GiGi, they brought gifts," Gracie whispered.

GiGi smiled and took her fingers like she was locking her lips and winked. She proceeded to the kitchen, and Gracie could hear that sweet belly laugh that she adored. "Come and get it, kids," GiGi announced.

"I believe Beau is our facilitator, so please, may I introduce the one, the only, Mr. Beau."

Everyone stood up and clapped, along with cat whistles. "Please hold your applause," Beau announced with that killer smile. "We are on a limited time schedule since most of us are on our lunch hours, so let's get on with the show. Girls, take it away."

"Please note that there are many small items, wrapped so beautifully by some, not so nicely wrapped by others," The group laughed, "Let's proceed to the ceremony of the opening of gifts. Gracie, you will notice that each gift has meaning. We are sure that you will know the meaning of each gift. Come on up here and let the celebration begin."

The group began jumping like popcorn and clapping wildly, hooting, and hollering as Gracie ran up front. "Remember, we only have an hour."

Gracie hurried through opening the gifts and could not believe what they all had brought her and such thoughtful gifts: suntan oil, beach towel, Starbucks card, writing pen with a starfish on it, journal with starfish on the cover, stamps, starfish stationery, beach chair, and Beau personally brought his gift up last.

Gracie was holding her breath as he walked toward her, his blue eyes looking right through her. She could feel her face blushing. He twirled her around, picked up his gift, and said, "Gracie, we are saving the best gift until last. The trick is that you cannot open it until tomorrow night, on the top of the Ferris Wheel accompanied by yours truly."

Gracie froze.

"Food is getting cold. Dig in, kids, and don't be late for work."

Saved again by GiGi, Gracie thought.

As Gracie watched the group ride away, she wondered where Beau had gone. One of the girls turned around and pointed over toward the back yard. Curiosity pulled her to the back yard. As she walked through the arbor, Beau surprised her, pulled her close and said, "I just wanted to tell you good-bye privately if that is okay with you?"

"Yes, sure," she whispered. She could feel her knees getting weak again and closed her eyes.

"I can't wait to see you tonight, Gracie. It's going to be a great night." With that said, he kissed her cheek.

She kept her eyes closed and felt Beau's soft lips on hers for a moment.

"Until tomorrow night."

"Until tomorrow night then," she answered.

Beau let her go and headed out to the road. He looked back and waved as he headed to town.

Those blue eyes are so hard to miss. Gracie

grabbed her heart. She waved and noticed that Beau had done the same thing, as he headed off back to town. *"What is happening?"* she asked herself. *"This is crazy!"*

Gracie went inside to help GiGi clean up the kitchen.

"It's all done, Luv!"

"You might want to rest some before you head out again with the wild bunch. I believe that's what they call the group at night?"

"Isn't there something else that I can help you with? Time is slipping away, and I have to head back to school soon," she said sadly.

"I have everything under control. All except for Mr. Blue Eyes!" GiGi laughed and went out the back door to the garden. "I almost forgot to feed the fish today," she said as she headed outside.

The phone started ringing and the Caller ID showed an UNKNOWN number.

"Can you get that, Luv?" GiGi hollered.

"Hello, Douglas residence."

"Gracie, this is Max. I miss you."

Gracie hung up the phone after a brief conversation and went straight upstairs to start another 4-cap bubble bath. This time, it would be accompanied by a small glass of wine and some good soft rock music.

Gracie sunk deep into the bubbles of the antique, claw-foot bathtub and thought about the words Max said. She told herself that she would not let it ruin her last night with GiGi, the wild bunch, and Beau.

She had much to do to prepare for the journey on Saturday morning. How she dreaded leaving.

She didn't want to see Max. She did not want to hash it out again. She hoped that the semester would fly, and she could return quickly.

The wine and bubbles were relaxing, and Gracie drifted off to sleep.

5

Gracie awoke many times during the night thinking about upcoming finals, leaving GiGi, Max, and Beau. How she longed to sit down with Mama to pour out her heart. She spent much of the night on her knees praying for God's direction and divine intervention at this crossroads of her life.

"Good morning, Luv. Time is passing quickly. What time are they picking you up this evening?"

"I think they will be here around 6 p.m. We are going to grab a bite at one of the beachside cafes, then head over to the pier to hear the band, ride the rides, and walk the beach one more time."

"Do you want to help me in the garden some and then maybe we'll hit town again for lunch before your big night tonight?"

"That would be great, GiGi. Would you like me to get those weeds out front, too?"

"That would be grand, Luv."

The time seemed to fly as they spent the day together talking about the past, the future, and the day. GiGi told Gracie that the beach house would be hers one day and she wanted her to know. Gracie was stunned and put her hand on GiGi's.

"GiGi…"

"That's what your mama wanted, Luv."

Gracie's eyes widened as she thought of so many things. "I don't know what to say, GiGi."

"Well, it's 4:45, you know."

"Okay, thanks, GiGi. Time has gotten away from me. What are you doing tonight? Do you want to come along with us?"

GiGi laughed that great belly laugh and said, "I don't think I could keep up with all of you!"

"I know you could, GiGi, probably better than me."

Gracie finished the weeding out front and hurried to get ready and tried to think about what to wear. Cutoffs and one of Mama's old t-shirts seemed to fit the bill. She saw Mama's ring that she had given her laying on the dresser. *"I believe I need to wear that as well,"* she thought to herself and slipped it on. It fit perfectly.

"I see them coming," GiGi exclaimed. "Looks like they are all dressed like you, ha!"

"That's good news. I wasn't sure what to expect from the bicycle group!" Gracie and GiGi laughed and headed out to the front porch.

"Well, she didn't back out, Beau," one group member shouted out. They all began to laugh.

"See you soon, GiGi," Gracie said as she walked out to get on her bike.

"I doubt it," GiGi said quietly to herself.

"What, GiGi?"

"Oh, nothing. See you later. Have fun."

Beau peddled up by Gracie's bike and said, "Let's get this show on the road. The race is on."

"Here we go!" Gracie thought.

"Here we go!" Beau thought.

The company and food were great. The water was crystal blue and beautiful. Gracie could understand why GiGi stayed here. The salty air, the seagulls, the warm breezes, the sun shining on the water like diamonds. So much to take in and not much time left.

"Hey, we will be here in time for the sunset! Let's walk over to the pier. Gracie needs some tourist photos to take back to school with her."

Gracie looked down and was so surprised by how Beau seemed to know so much about her in the brief time that they had met. "How did you guess, Beau?"

Beau looked at her and said quietly so only she could hear, "I pay attention and want to know everything about you."

Gracie looked up at him and thought, *"Oh, my..."*

"There you go again, Twinkle."

The group scurried over to the pier and began taking crazy group photos. A fisherman on the dock volunteered to take pictures of the group. It was so much fun. The sun setting in the background made great photos. Gracie knew she would love looking at them and remembering all the great times when she went back to school.

"I'd like to wait to ride the Ferris wheel until dark if that is okay with you, Gracie?" Beau asked. "You can see so much at night with all the lights… and stars."

"That's my favorite time to ride, too."

"Until then, guys. Let's head over to the go carts and the roller coaster!"

"Let's go!"

The group headed over and had a blast. The ticket taker was a former classmate and allowed them all to ride longer than normal since it was a slow night. They could hear the band in the background beginning to play.

"Hey, it's time for some mus-sac. Let's head over after the Tilt-a-Whirl."

Beau touched Gracie's hand and asked, "May I have this dance? It's my favorite song."

Gracie could feel her face blushing and her heart racing. She knew all the words. "Well, of course."

Beau pulled her close and their bodies fit so perfectly and danced in perfect time. Gracie could smell Beau's fresh scent which she loved. Beau rubbed his cheek on Gracie's hair.

"I love your hair, Gracie."

Gracie squeezed him and said, "Thanks, Beau." She closed her eyes and held on. Never had she felt so safe and happy.

Someone snapped a quick picture of them and asked, "Okay if I send this to you? It's a good one."

"Sure," they both answered in unison and laughed.

The song ended, and Gracie did not want to let go.

"Our next song is another slow one. Hold onto your dance partner a little longer. Here we go!" the band leader announced.

"Thank goodness!" Gracie thought.

"I wish this night could last forever," Beau said.

"I was just thinking the same thing."

When the song ended, Beau said, "I think it's time for the Ferris wheel. Are you up for it, gang?"

"You bet we are."

As they headed over to the ride, Gracie noticed Beau pulling something out of his pocket. It was a beautifully wrapped gift. "This is for you, Twinkle, but we have to wait until we get to the top before you can open it. I'll hold it for you until then."

"All right."

When they handed the tickets to the ride operator, Beau handed him two extra tickets. "Do you mind letting us stay on top for a while so we can look at the stars? Tonight, is Gracie's last night and she wants to get a couple good photos before heading back."

"No problem. You've got it, Beau," he said with a huge grin. "I will also let you off last."

Beau gave him a high five and guided Gracie onto the ride.

"This is going to be great getting to ride with you, Gracie. I haven't been on one of these for years."

Beau helped Gracie get on the seat and slid in beside her and put his arm around her. "Is this okay? I don't want you to fall out," he smiled.

It was a perfect night. The stars were shining so brightly, and Beau pointed out landmarks seen from high above. He also pointed out Orion's Belt, the Big and Little Dippers, as well as other constellations.

"I just wanted to tell you that none of those compare to you, Gracie. I really have been waiting for a girl like you."

"I wish I didn't have to leave."

"I feel the same, but maybe you will want to come back for the summer?" He squeezed her a little tighter and brushed her hair from her face to look in her eyes. "I really want you to come back, Gracie. Promise me that you will."

"I promise, Beau."

Suddenly she felt herself falling like she never had before. How could this be? They just met. They continued in silence and then the operator stopped the ride with them on top.

Beau reached into his pocket and said, "Here's your present, Gracie. I hope you like it." It was a small box, wrapped in royal blue and aqua paper with a beautiful matching bow.

"Do you want me to open it now?"

"Yes."

Gracie's hands trembled as she opened the tiny box. "Where did you find this? It matches the ring that GiGi gave me that belonged to my mom."

"My dad had bought them for your mom and wasn't able to give them to her."

Gracie felt a tiny tear well up in her eye.

"I have saved them for all this time hoping to find someone like you to give it to."

"Beau, it's so beautiful."

"I found this postcard, too. GiGi told me it's our parents on the front."

"Beau." Gracie reached over and touched his face, and he kissed her so sweetly.

"I am so glad that we met. I just never dreamed that…" Beau stopped in mid-sentence.

"I know. I didn't either."

GiGi had told me that when they used to ride the Ferris wheel together. They would always say a rhyme that your mom wrote. It went something like this:

Up high on a Ferris wheel at the edge of the sea,
Starry skies and moonlight with your arms wrapped around me.

"I found a postcard that was never sent to your dad with those words on the back. I love it, Beau. This night, this gift, and you are so special."

Beau leaned down again and kissed her forehead, then her hair. "I won't forget your scent, Gracie."

They sat there in silence for a bit, embracing with eyes closed. Just then a shooting star fell from the sky.

"Make a wish."

"I already have," he said smiling. "Make your wish and this summer, when you come back, you will have to tell me what your wish was. Deal?"

"Deal."

The Ferris wheel started again. They both sighed at the same time and then laughed aloud.

"The group is down at the beach. Want to go down there with them or head back?"

"I don't want this night to end."

"Neither do I."

* * *

Gracie and Beau slowly walked to join the group at the beach without talking, hands clasped so tightly.

"It's hard to believe that tonight is your last night,

Gracie. It seems like you have always been here."

"I know what you mean."

"Have you decided about the summer yet? No pressure, of course," one of the girls asked.

"I am sure to return. I think I would miss you all too much."

"We thought so," the group said in unison. With those words, Beau picked Gracie up and threw her over his shoulders and ran to the water. The group followed, and they all participated in a huge water fight at the edge of the sea.

Exhausted, they all fell on their backs in the sand and stared up at the stars. Gracie almost felt as if she needed to pinch herself. She hadn't felt this happy for such a long time. Maybe never.

* * *

Beau rolled over on his side so he could see Gracie's face. Gracie turned on her side to face Beau. They did not utter a word, but the silence spoke volumes.

"Guys, we'd better get Gracie home. She has a long drive tomorrow and needs to pack still. Am I right?"

"Yes, you are right. I do have quite a bit to do tonight, and I need to spend time with GiGi. I will be heading out of town about five a.m. tomorrow morning."

Everyone stood up and huddled around Gracie. "I'd say it's time for a big, long group hug. Are you up to it? Beau asked.

"I definitely am. I cannot wait to get back here to

see you all."

They hugged Gracie very tightly, and Beau leaned in and gave her a quick kiss on the cheek.

Beau smiled and wrapped his towel around Gracie and said, "Let's get you home."

The walk home was quiet. Beau talked a bit about the constellations, the Milky Way, and other things that Gracie did not remember. What she did remember was the way Beau wrapped his towel around her and looked in her eyes in a way that made her feel as if she had always known him and that he was someone who really got her.

"Well, here we are. I don't want to let go of your hand, because I know it's going to be awhile before I see you again." Gracie smiled and reached up to hug Beau again.

The porch light came on and GiGi stepped out of the screen door. "Did you kids have a fun time tonight? And did you convince Gracie to come back for the summer?"

"I'll let her answer that, and I had better be going. It has been a pleasure meeting and getting to know you, Gracie."

"Thank you for everything, Beau. You have been so kind. Goodnight."

"Goodnight, Beau! See you tomorrow," GiGi said. "Don't look so surprised, Gracie. I have more work in the garden for Beau." She cackled and turned around and went inside.

Beau turned around, waved to Gracie, and disappeared into the darkness.

Gracie threw him a kiss after his back was turned and she thought to herself, *"What did I just do? This is crazy!*

"It has been a wonderful week having you here. You just seem to make this beach house come alive."

"I sure hate to leave, but my finals are right around the corner, and I have not studied much at all. It sure was worth it though," Gracie said with a smile.

GiGi smiled too. "What can I do to help you, Luv?"

* * *

Gracie finished packing around one a.m. after drinking hot tea with GiGi. She snuggled down under the patchwork quilt on the bed and thought of the wonderful week, her new friends, GiGi, and Beau. She felt as if Mama was lying there beside her like the old days. Hugging her pillow, she felt she could almost smell Mama's perfume on it. Could it still be there after all this time? Gracie longed to tell Mama about it all.

Gracie noticed Mama's Bible on the nightstand. She took it with her everywhere. Everything happened so fast, losing Mama. Gracie thought back to those last days with her. No one realized that Mama's last day at home would be so treasured and the outcome so unexpected. Gracie remembered getting the call that Mama was not doing well and to come quickly to see her. Sitting by Mama's bed while she laid there unresponsive, Gracie held Mama's hand to warm it. It was so cold. Mama seemed to be asleep. The minutes seemed like hours sitting there with her, hoping for a change. Gracie covered Mama up, kissed her, and told her that she loved her. Before she could return the next morning, Mama was gone. She had begun her journey to her new home in heaven.

The days and weeks that followed seemed to be a blur with all the appointments and things to take care of for Mama. Gracie thought of Mama's Bible and all the things that she kept in it. Things that meant so much. She was so glad that she had it. It always made her seem closer to Mama and God when reading and meditating on Mama's favorite scripture, Psalm 139, "You have searched me, Lord, and you know me."

That particular scripture and following verses always seemed to calm Gracie when she needed it most.

Mama's Bible even had a page torn out from Grandma Sophie's Bible showing each person in their family and their names, date, and place where they received salvation. "March 1993 in the basement of the Baptist church was when Mama received Christ." Mama had penciled in the date that Gracie accepted Christ.

Another treasure that Mama had left behind, Gracie thought as she began her prayers before falling off to sleep.

6

Four a.m. came early. Gracie got up and tried her best not to wake GiGi. As she began brushing her teeth, a familiar voice said, "I am already up, so you don't have to be quiet! What would you like for breakfast, Luv? French toast or biscuits and gravy?"

"Coffee sure sounds good right now," Gracie laughed. "It seems I am leaving with more than I came with."

"Always, Dear."

Gracie turned around to refocus on closing her suitcase when she noticed something in her car outside her window. She tried to see what it was, but it was still too dark outside.

"I think I'll take my suitcase out and get the car packed. Be right back." As she came upon the car, she noticed there was a flower or plant inside. She tossed her suitcase in the trunk and opened the passenger door to see a beautiful lily plant in the passenger seat with a seatbelt around it. The card attached read:

My Dear Twinkle,

We have had a wonderful week and I look forward to spending the summer with you. Since I know you have such a love for music and classic rock, I have included some classic rock songs for you to listen to on your way back to school and

on your way back here soon.
Until I see you again,
Beau

Gracie hurried back inside to eat with GiGi and to tell her good-bye. As she headed down the road, she stopped at the beach near the Ferris Wheel and thought of her sweet Mama and the postcard.

Gracie was so glad that GiGi had shared the sweet story of Mama and Beau's father. Even though they didn't end up together, Mama and he had wonderful memories of their time together growing up. Gracie felt that these souvenirs – the postcard, the ring, the message in a bottle — were like a treasure map that led her to Beau. Gracie hoped that she would get to meet Beau's parents when she returned this summer.

Time would tell. Hurry, summer!

* * *

As Gracie headed down the highway, she smiled to herself and knew the last month of school and finals would fly by. She knew she could graduate early if she attended summer school. Her thoughts took her back to the Bicycle Club mentioning taking summer classes on the beach. It really wasn't too tough of a decision. She knew that would be the right thing for her.

Max called her as she was enroute back. He had their summer planned in Europe. Gracie had no plans to fly to Europe and chase him around, waiting, waiting, always waiting. She planned to stay busy and spend as much time in the library studying as she could because Max was always disrupting and interrupting every plan she made. He finally got the message when he told her that he had bought a plane ticket for her, and she told him to get a refund for it.

Max was in shock and quiet. She told him that he had hurt her too many times to think things might be different this time and she knew it would not make any difference being in Europe. Max told her he would be leaving the day after graduation for his new job across the pond. Gracie wished him well and told him this was good-bye.

Max said, "I'm sorry, Gracie. I had no idea that you felt this way."

Gracie said, "Goodbye, Max. Please know that I truly wish the best for you."

Gracie had her summer already planned. She would enroll in online summer classes so she could graduate, pack her car, and head back to the beach on the last day of school. She could not wait to get back there.

As Gracie drove away, GiGi flickered the front porch light three times. GiGi heard a "Honk, honk, honk" then returned to the kitchen to finish her coffee. As she sat down, she began thinking about her daughter, Joy, and her beautiful smile. This led her to thoughts of Beau's father and how sweet the two were together. It just was not meant to be. Who would have thought an old postcard would have brought about so many questions. Questions that GiGi knew she would have to answer someday soon.

GiGi took her coffee out to the porch and noticed a small note on the table between their wicker rocking chairs.

"GiGi, thank you for everything and especially the cinnamon rolls. I saved this last one for you. Love, Gracie."

With that, GiGi reached for a fork and settled in enjoying her morning coffee and cinnamon roll. The sun began rising on the shoreline with a beautiful silver and gold outline as it rose, peaking in and out of the clouds on the journey across the sky. Just then two dolphins seemed to be playing tag along the edge of the beach. GiGi enjoyed watching them so much. It made her think of Papa and his old truck. She couldn't let go of his things and still wore his faded denim work shirts when there was a chill in the air. She continued to rock and think of the days gone by and how she loved him with all her heart. She sighed and thought, *"I'll drink another cup this morning for Papa, because, after all – he always made the best coffee."*

* * *

Beau felt a little melancholy thinking of Gracie going back to school. He hoped time would go quickly for both of them. He knew in his heart that she would come back. None of this made sense, and he didn't understand any of it. He thought about her smile and the way she looked at him. He knew this was different than anything he had experienced before in his life.

* * *

Gracie decided to drive up the shoreline back to school even though it took longer. She had so much to do and prayed the time would go quickly. The shorebirds and pelicans followed her up the coastline as she drove north. Max called again as she was driving home, but she did not answer. She wanted to focus on the future and not the past. She remembered then that Beau had left the CD for her to listen to. Song #1 – "Seagull." She couldn't believe it and began to sing along.

* * *

Max was astounded the way Gracie was acting toward him. She had always been so easy going and now she wouldn't even answer a call or text? He wondered what had changed but was confident that he could work it all out with her like he always did. He knew he hadn't always been the best boyfriend, but Gracie was always there. He decided to drive by Gracie's apartment to see if she was back. He wanted to give her his gift from Europe. He then remembered it had been an exceedingly long time since he bought her anything.

* * *

Gracie arrived back at her apartment and carried her bags in, along with all the treasures she received while she was away. The weather was cold and rainy. She gathered up her books and headed to the library to study, thinking no one would look for her there. Just then, there was a knock at the door. Oh no! she thought. Looking through the glass, she could see it was Max. How she dreaded opening the door.

"Be right there."

"Okay, it's Max. I can't wait to see you!"

Gracie opened the door and Max scooped her up in a big six foot five bearhug.

"I'm so glad to see you! I brought you a gift from

my trip. Here you go!"

"Max, you didn't need to do that."

"I wanted to. Here, let me help you. Come and sit down by me."

As Gracie opened the beautifully wrapped box, she gasped, "Max!" It was a one carat diamond.

"I had planned to fly you out to propose to you in Paris, but we weren't able to connect."

"Max, I don't know what to say."

"Well, it's now or never, Gracie. What's it going to be?"

Just then, Gracie received a text message from her best friend, Julie. It read, "Hey, I'm glad you will be home soon. Call me when you get in so we can catch up AND I am sorry to have seen Max with some girl from France this past week. I guess that means you are no longer together?" *"Perfect timing,"* Gracie thought to herself and subconsciously grimaced.

"What was that for?" Max asked.

"What?"

"That face?"

"Here you go. Any thoughts on this text I just received from Julie?"

"I was just showing the girl around while she was here visiting."

"Does the girl have a name?"

"What does it matter now?"

"You're always full of surprises, aren't you?" Gracie asked. "I'm really tired and need to get a paper finished for my class tomorrow. Do you mind if we finish this conversation later?" *"Or not at all,"* she thought to herself.

Max tried to force a hug, then a kiss. Gracie backed away and could feel the same disappointment all over her face. Gracie said, "I really have to go now and do not have peace about any of it." Gracie ran out the door before Max could stop her. "Good-bye, Max. You can let yourself out," she hollered.

"Gracieeeeeee!"

* * *

Gracie texted Julie and asked her to meet her at the library. When she arrived, Julie was already there.

"What's the scoop?"

"I saw him holding hands and walking with a petite, dark-haired girl about a week ago. That's all I know."

Another stab to the heart. Gracie remembered that Max always said he was not the type of guy to hold hands in public. Here's your sign, Gracie thought to herself. "I guess that's enough! Now tell me what you did during spring break. Are you going to be able to graduate this spring or summer?" Gracie asked.

The girls talked all about their spring breaks and all that they did. "Will you be staying to study here at the library tonight?" I've really got to get this paper completed by tomorrow morning."

"Yes, I've got some projects to get started on that are due in a couple weeks."

"Good, let's get this show on the road," Gracie said and tried to smile. *"More confirmation,"* Gracie thought to herself.

The hours seemed to pass quickly while

completing the paper. Around midnight, Gracie asked, "Are you going to stay here all night? I am going to head home and finish editing there. How about you?" Gracie asked, crossing her eyes.

"I'm almost at a good stopping point. Give me fifteen and we can leave at the same time, okay? Julie asked.

Gracie started gathering up her things and started to think about Max's Now or Never comment. Just makes sense now. She wondered what GiGi or Mama would think about all of this. Of course, they both would tell her to get down on her knees and pray.

"Ready if you are, "Julie whispered. "How about a midnight snack?"

Gracie laughed and said, "I'm in!" They both laughed and headed toward the Food Court. It looked as if they were closing.

"Are we thinking tacos or burgers?" Julie asked, then at the same time, they both said, "Breakfast!" They chuckled and decided to drive to get breakfast.

After the quick snack, both girls hurried home to prepare for the next day. Gracie had a little more work to finalize her paper and planned to take a long bubble bath after that. *Lots of bubbles tonight and a glass of wine or a shot of tequila,"* she thought.

Five text messages started rolling in. Gracie wanted to turn her phone off. Much to her surprise, there was one text from GiGi, three from Max, and one from Beau. She immediately read GiGi and Beau's texts. They both wanted to be sure she made it home ok. She acknowledged that she made it and told them both she would call them on the weekend. Max's texts were left unread.

* * *

Gracie decided to call Beau first when she awoke.
"Hello there!"
"Gracie?"
"It's a good thing you gave me your number when I was there so I could call you, ha!"
They both laughed and talked about their day and upcoming week ahead. Beau told Gracie that he makes it a point to ride by GiGi's house every day to wave at her on the porch. Gracie loved that about Beau.
"Will I see you in a month or so?"
"You can count on it, Beau. I am hoping to finish this summer with online classes to graduate. Can you believe it. I didn't realize I was so close!"
"Congratulations. I am not surprised," Beau happily stated.
"Are you close to graduating, too?"
"Well, since you asked, I am finishing this semester!"
"We will have a lot to celebrate, won't we?"
"We sure will. I'll see you soon, Twinkle."
"'Bye!"
Gracie felt that heart tug again. Whew! She hurried to call GiGi and was glad to hear her voice. GiGi asked Gracie to house-sit in June and July due to scheduling an Alaskan cruise with GiGi's sister, Aunt Ginny and brother, Uncle John. Gracie thought she might invite Julie and some friends down while GiGi was gone. Julie had been there to the cottage before and

absolutely loved it.

"I will be graduating at the end of the summer. Can you believe it, GiGi?"

"Your mama and dad would have been so proud! Papa, too!"

"It has gone pretty quickly!"

"What will you do after graduation, Luv?"

"I'm not sure."

"I hope it's somewhere close to here, you know, if it works out for you." GiGi hoped she wasn't being too pushy. "Your uncle may be contacting you eventually about working for him at his publishing house in the city. When he found out your major was Journalism, he hoped to speak with you before we leave on the cruise. Remember when we used to visit there? What do you think?"

"Hmmmm, sounds interesting." Gracie remembered the stacks of books and hiding from her great uncle. Everyone was so nice and kind there and seemed to genuinely love their jobs. Uncle John was a great boss. Employees with smiles and lots of demanding work. She wondered if it would still be like that there.

7

The whole month of May passed so quickly, and Gracie was glad. She was counting down the days until she could feel her feet in the warm sand again. Thoughts of Beau kept her on track to get things completed and get out of there! She had packed up her apartment and gave most of her things away. She wanted to start fresh and looked forward to the future that God had in store for her. She had faith that He was leading her steps and was preparing the way for her. When the last day of school finally came, Gracie packed her car with all that would fit. She had been given Mama's convertible Spyder, so she couldn't bring much with her.

How she loved her mama's car. The guardian angel was still on the visor that mama had placed there when Gracie first received her driver's license. Gracie had all that she needed – her clothes, overnight bag, and the souvenirs from the spring break.

There were parties and so much going on, but Gracie had no interest in any of it, mainly because she did not want to run into Max anywhere. Gracie said her goodbyes to all her college friends and headed south to the sunshine. She did not return any of Max's texts and didn't want him to know she was leaving today. She remembered that he would be leaving the next day for Europe. She didn't feel like there was much more to say.

She drove through the drive thru to get a large coffee for the drive south and hoped to take the Coastal Highway when she got closer. Windows down, top down, sunglasses on, and the CD in the player that Beau had made her. What a great start to the rest of her life.

Gracie was thankful the weather was beautiful and clear for the trip south without bumper-to-bumper traffic. When she reached the Coastal Highway, she felt she was home. She pulled over to take a few pictures and thought she might use them for a "cover-page" someday or send them in to a photograph contest. *"Only God knows the desires of our hearts,"* she thought. One more hour from there. Gracie pulled in to gas up and get another beverage and thought she would text GiGi to let her know she was not far away.

* * *

At last, Gracie felt as if she were home as she drove through town. Things were hopping due to the beginning of the tourist season there. She could see boats in the harbor checking their sails and summer help swabbing the decks. The flowers in the hanging baskets on the city light poles were full of color. She drove down the main street and once around the square and hoped to see Beau out running errands as she drove through. No Beau in sight, but she did see GiGi's truck parked by the Seaside market and guessed she was preparing for supper tonight. A little farther down the street, she saw a group of bicycles near the bookstore. Gracie figured they were all ordering their books for summer classes. Beau had said that the bookstore was great to order any book that a person needed, especially students of all ages. "Lifelong learning is where it's at," Beau would say. This thought reminded Gracie that she would like to take the online Master Gardener's class through the County Extension this winter and hoped GiGi would take it with her.

Gracie decided to head on to the house to start unloading so she could get settled in. As she began carrying her things inside, she noticed a note from GiGi. It read:

"Hello Luv! So glad you are home. Your room is ready, and I have put a new quilt that you haven't seen on your bed that was made by Grandma Sophie. I am anxious to see what you think! The pattern is "North Star." I had to run in to town to get some things for dinner tonight and need to pick up a few last-minute items for my trip to Alaska, so make yourself at home. There is chocolate sheet cake on the counter and the coffee is ready – just hit start. Ha-ha! See you soon, Dear. Love, GiGi"

Gracie ran up the stairs to see the quilt. It was so beautiful with Gracie's favorite colors and was handstitched, of course. She knew it took hours and days to do this. Gracie then remembered that as Grandma Sophie began to get older, she would spend one-third of the year at GiGi's and the other two-thirds at Uncle John's and Aunt Ginny's. Grandma Sophie would handpiece each quilt block, then piece that top together. Once completed, GiGi would gather materials to place on the quilt racks, and they would invite GiGi's friends over to complete the quilt. They would have such fun at their quilt parties in front of the huge bay window in view of the beach. Each friend would bring finger foods and they would cackle, and they laughed and told jokes and stories. There were a few times while visiting that Mama and Gracie were invited to participate in the masterpieces. Gracie cherished these memories so. She felt so blessed.

Honk, honk! GiGi was home! Gracie slid down the banister and hurried out to see GiGi and to help carry in the goodies!

"It looks like you bought out the store!"

"I sure did and got some of your favorites."

"Here, let me help, GiGi. I can get it all."

"Thank you, Luv. I'll head in and start fixing lunch for us."

As Gracie began loading up, she heard a group yelling her name from afar. She looked up and it was some of the girls from the group she had met during spring break. Gracie put the bags down and waved with both arms to make sure they knew she heard them. Before long, they had made it up the drive, wheels smoking on their bikes.

"Hey girls! So glad to see you!

"We are glad you are here. We're getting together this weekend at the pier and hope you can come along, too."

"I'm fairly sure I will be free. I will need to check in with GiGi to see when her ship leaves. She is going to Alaska for a bit with her sister and brother. How fun is that?"

"Sounds like a dream! They will have a blast. We

can see you are busy and will be in touch. Bye!"

"See you later!"

Gracie carried the items inside to be put away. She stopped on the porch for a minute and gazed at the sea. The sound of the emerald waters was so calming.

"Just bring everything in here, Dear."

"Okay. GiGi, I love the quilt! It's my favorite colors too!"

"I thought you would," she said with a smile. "It was one that your mother and you helped with long ago."

"Well, that makes it even more special!"

"Let's get all of this put away so I can hear how your last few weeks of school went."

After all the groceries were placed in the cabinets and refrigerator, GiGi said, "Grab your lunch and let's sit on the porch."

"Can I get you some coffee or something cold to drink?"

"Coffee would be perfect, thank you! Now catch me up on what has been going on! More importantly, I want to hear how you were able to graduate so quickly!"

Gracie began telling how the Registrar had revised her transfer credits which placed her over what she needed to graduate. Gracie thought she would have to take elective classes over the summer to complete her degree, but as it turned out, she didn't need to. She was so happy.

"And Max?"

"Oh boy, GiGi, you wouldn't believe it."

Gracie explained all that had happened and how

she was so glad to be here.

GiGi said, "I'm glad you're here too, Luv. Now about this cruise!" GiGi showed Gracie the itinerary for the trip starting June 1st and ending July 31st.

"You're going to be gone 2 months?"

"Can you take care of everything for me while I am gone? I didn't think you would mind."

"No, of course, it's ok. I just didn't realize you would be gone that length of time. Good for you!"

"I am so looking forward to spending time with my family. It has been years since we were all together for any length of time. They will be here this weekend to discuss our travel plans and, of course, to see you."

"I haven't seen them since Mama's funeral. It will be good to see them."

"You are their only great-niece, so they are so anxious to hear what is new with you. It is sad that neither of them had any children. They always happily focused on your mother and you."

"They always remembered our birthdays, Christmas, and any other special occasions and would call and send a card. Their wonderful gifts usually bought my books for the next semester. They were so generous and thoughtful. You three are the three musketeers for sure! I cannot wait to see them! They won't be here Friday night, will they?"

"No, they are coming Sunday and your uncle has special orders for chicken and noodles for lunch, so Saturday. I will be rolling out noodles and might need your help. What do you say?"

"I'm looking forward to that! Do we have

anything planned for Friday night?"

"Hmmm, does the gang have something planned already? You just got here, girl!"

"Yes, I know. They are always doing something and invited me to meet them at the pier if you and I didn't have anything planned."

"We don't have anything planned. Sounds like fun!"

"Okay, great! I'll let them know!"

8

Sunday seemed to roll around quickly after Friday night at the pier and Saturday preparing noodles and food for Aunt Ginny and Uncle John. GiGi was up early preparing homemade yeast rolls and the final additions.

"Hey, girlie, can you finish setting the table for me?"

"Of course! Oh, it is so beautiful! Fresh flowers from GiGi's flower garden lined the middle of the table from GiGi's flower garden. "Are we using the good China dishes today? The blue willow set?"

"Well, yes," GiGi said as she whirled around to set the cake and pies on the antique buffet. Another treasure of Grandma Sophie's.

"Looks like we are feeding an army!"

GiGi winked and said, "I thought we might need a little extra in case we have friends stop by later on this evening."

Gracie hoped so because Beau was out of town with family on Friday and Saturday, and she had not seen him yet. She began imagining his eyes and smile.

"Gracie, it looks like you have quite a bit of flour on your shirt. Where is your apron, Dear?"

"I'm going to run on up and change. I'd hate to get this all over them, ha."

Once Gracie made it up the stairs, the doorbell rang.

"They're here!"

"Who's that beautiful girl?" Uncle John bellowed. This always made Gracie blush.

"Uncle John!" He began to chuckle as he always did and then they all began to laugh.

Lunch was fabulous, and Aunt Ginny and Uncle John had so many questions for Gracie regarding graduation, after graduation plans, and everything else that one could imagine.

"GiGi, I'll get the dishes so you all can go over the itinerary for your big Alaskan excursion. You have so much to plan and talk about! Anyone ready for coffee?"

They all answered, "Yes!"

"Are we waiting on dessert until all the plans are made then?"

In unison, they all said, "Yes!"

"Is there an echo in the room?" Gracie smiled and said as she began pouring the coffee.

"Gracie, when we're through with our trip discussion, I'd like to chat more with you about your after graduation plans even though it's only been less than a week - on your timeline, of course," Uncle John said.

"Yes, of course, Uncle John!"

Gracie was anxious to get the table cleared and dishes washed and put away for GiGi. "I'm going for a quick walk down the beach and will be back soon, ok? It looks like you are up to your elbows in seals, walruses, and polar bears. See you in a bit."

Gracie grabbed her sunglasses and headed down the beach path. *"It sure feels good to be home again,"* Gracie thought. She was gone for about 30 minutes and returned to see that the group had finished their planning session.

"Come on in here and tell us about your post-graduation plans. What's your short and long-term thoughts? Wasn't your major Journalism and minor in Graphic Art?" Aunt Ginny asked.

"Yes, do tell! We are all ears and listening attentively!" GiGi said.

Before Gracie could speak, Uncle John said, "I have a spot for an editor and research assistant at my company if you might be remotely interested. It may be contracted work to begin though."

"Interested? I would love to hear more about this. Everything I had planned has seemed to abruptly change. I have felt that I need to be here at this time instead of running off to Europe," Gracie said.

"Jeremiah 29:11?"

"Exactly, Uncle John!"

"Send your resume to me tomorrow. Once I receive it, HR will call to discuss the position more in detail and set up an interview."

"I will send it tonight. Thank you for giving me the opportunity to apply, Uncle John."

"You're welcome, Gracie."

"Well, I guess I will see you all next week!" Gracie said.

"We are so looking forward to this trip. It's been such a long time since we were all together," Aunt

Ginny said.

"Come in for a group hug and selfie before you go!" Gracie pulled everyone together on the porch and took the picture. "This is a great picture!"

"Send it to us!" Uncle John said.

"I just did," Gracie said with a smile.

As they drove away, Aunt Ginny hollered out the window, "We'll see you in a few days!"

GiGi and Gracie stood on the porch and waved until they could no longer see them.

"I guess I must start packing. I may have to buy some new warmer clothing!"

"GiGi, if you are needing warmer clothes, I have too many! Please come upstairs and take what you like. We are the same size."

"I am getting so excited. Let's go!" GiGi said and she hurried up the stairs.

"You are in such great shape, GiGi. Thank you for the great genes!"

"You're welcome, Luv."

GiGi began trying on the clothing with Gracie's approval. Within the hour, GiGi's suitcase was almost packed.

"I'll grab a few more things for the old suitcase and meet you on the beach for a short walk, ok?"

"I'm already there," Gracie beamed.

As they walked the beach, Gracie and GiGi talked about their memories on the beach.

"I hope you will be walking this beach someday with your little girl or boy," GiGi said.

"Me, too, with you maneuvering the construction

of the best sandcastles. I brought you a surprise for all those shells that we have collected through the years."

"What is it, Luv?"

"You'll see. If I told you now, it wouldn't be a surprise."

"Well, I think I am ready to head back now then!"

They both laughed and hurried back to the cottage.

"Here you go!"

The surprise was two glass-based lamps to which GiGi could add her favorite shells to.

"Oh my! I have always wanted one."

"Well, good, because I bought you two and thought you might place them on the antique entryway table. What do you think?"

"I think we need to start getting those babies filled up!" GiGi said with a huge smile.

As they began to fill up the glass lamps, GiGi remembered a time on the beach when Mama was a little girl.

"Your mama always loved to hear the roar of the ocean in the large conch shells. She always said it was how the mermaids would call each other. She always hoped she would hear something back and would spend so much time calling out to them. She always had a couple in the secret garden. Do you remember?"

"I sure do. Mama had such an imagination! I loved the beachside paintings."

"She always had a conch shell in her beach paintings by her name. Did you notice?"

Gracie walked over the extra-large painting by

the 100-gallon fish tank and whirled around and said, "I did notice it in my favorites!" *"Another souvenir,"* Gracie thought. How she loved the memories that GiGi would share about her mom.

"GiGi, I will remember this story and share it with my little one someday."

Gracie put her arm around her sweet grandma and gave her a squeeze.

"I'm going to miss you while you are gone on your excursions."

GiGi leaned in and kissed Gracie on the cheek.

"Now how about some dinner, Luv? Are you up for Sophie's Special tonight?"

"Always," Gracie said.

9

The next morning, Gracie was up early for her daily morning walk on the beach. GiGi would laugh and say that it was those nice walks on the beach that kept her in such good shape. As she was walking, she received a text from Beau. "Hi there! We will be home late tomorrow evening. Is it ok if I stop by around seven?"

Gracie quickly texted back and said, "I look forward to seeing you soon!" She thought about the summer and what all was ahead of her then remembered she needed to send her resume to her uncle. She hastened her pace to get back in a record forty-five minutes. GiGi was out in the garden and Gracie hollered, "I'm back!" and headed upstairs. She received an immediate response from Uncle John with a message. "Glad to receive your resume! As we discussed, HR will be contacting you later today with the date and time of your interview. See you soon! You will have lunch after the interview with the Dept. Manager and HR Manager." Gracie quickly responded that she looked forward to the interview! She began looking in her closet to determine what she would wear to the interview. She knew she must present herself well and pulled out a navy suit with navy pumps. It just happened to match her navy leather file bag. *"This should do,"* she thought. She printed out four copies of her resume for the interview, along with references and contact info. *"Here we go,"* she thought." She considered the option that if she didn't receive an offer, she might find an opportunity at the bookstore while she was job searching. She began to get extremely excited about working in her actual field and prayed that God would make it so.

    Gracie had done research for a local publishing house at college and authored a few short stories for the college paper. She also had a great idea for her someday novel. She walked over and looked at the old manual typewriter in the hallway which belonged to Grandma Sophie. Grandma Sophie wrote for the local newspaper and penned some poetry in her spare time. GiGi organized Grandma Sophie's poems and had them bound into a little booklet which was displayed by the old typewriter. The cover of the booklet was Grandma Sophie standing on a stool, brushing her great grandmother's hair. Her great-grandmother, Kathryn, was sitting in the tiny sewing rocker displayed by the table. Gracie had read the poetry many times and loved her expressive and artistic soul. She felt so blessed to have such a wonderful heritage. She would never take that for granted.

    "What you up to, Luv?"

    "I just finished sending off my resume to Uncle John."

    "That's great. Any responses yet?"

    "I'm waiting on HR to set everything up, then will have lunch with the HR and the Dept. Manager afterwards. What do you have planned the rest of the day?"

"If my dear neighbor Olivia agrees, I will need to get home care set up for her before I leave for my trip. She doesn't have anyone to look in on her.

"What about the local assisted living facility? Would she agree to that?"

"I can ask. I think she would prefer to stay at home with the local Home Health Agency looking in on her. She gets around pretty well for one hundred years old!"

"I can look in on her wherever she is. I had no idea she was that age! She seems much younger than that."

"It's the salty air, Dear. See what you have to look forward to?"

Gracie smiled and gave her grandmother a squeeze. "I sure hope so."

10

Beau showed up promptly at seven p.m. Gracie and GiGi were sitting on the porch with a pitcher of fresh lemonade and cookies. Gracie expected him to bicycle over, but he drove his jeep this time.

"How's my two best girls?"

"Better now, "Gracie quickly answered. "Where's your bike?"

"It's in the back. I thought I'd show you a new path after we drink some of Grandma Sophie's secret lemonade recipe."

"How did you know it's Grandma Sophie's recipe?"

GiGi smiled and looked at Beau.

"Because I've had it before, ha."

"I'll go ahead and load your bike, so we can get going before the sun sets."

"It's fine," GiGi said as she looked at Gracie and smiled.

Beau quickly got up to load that bike.

Gracie whispered, "GiGi, was this already planned?"

"Well, maybe."

* * *

As Beau was loading the bike, Gracie went inside to get her bag with her phone. She came out and GiGi handed her a little picnic basket and winked.

"Here you go, Luv."

"Thank you, Mrs. Douglas. We won't be gone too long. Let's go, Gracie!"

Gracie climbed in the jeep and looked at Beau. "Where in the world are we going?"

"I have a secret path to show you. We could have ridden from here, but we are limited on time with the sun setting soon. You just turn left here and follow the grassy and gravel road along the beach, and it'll take you where we're going."

"Is that why the sign says Water's Edge Lane?" Gracie said as she nudged Beau.

"Come here, you!"

Beau put his arm around Gracie for a moment to give her a quick squeeze. As they winded down the road, there were many seagulls and wildlife present. Gracie was always in awe of the pattern of play that the seagulls had. If one seagull found a piece of grass or food, the others would chase them like they were playing a game of keep-a-way. The sun was beginning to set and the colors in the sky painted amber and magenta ribbons across the sky. Gracie took off her sunglasses.

"You sure don't see this every day up north, do you, Gracie?"

"No, you sure don't."

"Well, here we are!" Beau seemed overly excited and pulled both bikes out at the same time.

"What is that over there?"

"That is what I wanted to show you. We will

leave the bikes here for now. Beau said, "Come on" as he held out his hand to Gracie. Beau led her down a beach path with sea oats on both sides of the path and wildflowers scattered here and there. Gracie could see something that looked like an island with Adirondack chairs and fire pit close by.

"How did you find this place? It's spectacular!"

"I had been searching for something for quite some time. While you were back at school, it came up on the market and I decided to get it while I could. I have only brought a few people here, so you should know that you are one of the special ones."

"Do I dare ask who else has been here?"

"Only my parents, ha. They helped me finally decide to purchase it. It's my in-town getaway," Beau said quietly.

"I don't think you would ever want to leave here."

"I spent a lot of time here while you were away at school and said lots of prayers, Beau said shyly.

Gracie turned around and touched Beau's hand and said, "If your prayers were to bring me back, I am here."

Beau twirled Gracie around and they laughed, then he put his arms around her and said, "Would you look at that sunset!"

Gracie felt so at peace and content in that moment.

"Let's sit awhile. Did you bring GiGi's picnic basket?"

"Ta Dah! Here you go! It looks like there are

grapes, apples, cheese, and crackers. Oh look, GiGi threw in a small bottle of grape juice and two waters. She is amazing. Dig in!"

"This is so good, Gracie!

"Yes, it is!"

"Hey, do you see the dolphins over by the pier? It looks as if they are following a shrimp boat that is coming in for the night. See it?"

"Yes, and I see a mermaid following them!" Gracie snickered.

"You never know what you might see out here, Gracie!"

This made Gracie smile. She thought that nothing could be better than being here with Beau right now.

"Do you live nearby?"

"Yes, I have an apartment on my parent's estate, I mean land. It's small, but that is ok with me. Less to clean!"

"I sure get that. I guess I will stay with GiGi until I know what I will be doing in the next year. I wanted to tell you that I have an interview at my uncle's company this week."

"Will you have to move if or, I mean, when you get it?

"I'm not sure yet. I would rather commute if I can. Did you know that GiGi is going on an Alaskan Cruise with her siblings soon? She will be gone two months. "

"Yes, I have been hearing all about it. I know she is really looking forward to spending time with them. She would share a little about the trip when she would come in to get groceries."

"I'm so glad that they are going together. The three of them have not gone anywhere together in years."

"Hey, it's starting to get dark. Do you want to build a fire tonight?"

"Can I take a raincheck on that? I would love to, but with GiGi leaving soon, I feel I should spend more time with her."

"Yes, you are right. We need to get you home."

As they were packing up to leave, the moon and stars were beginning to rise.

Beau pointed up to the sky and asked, "What do you think of that?"

"I think I could get used to seeing this view quite easily."

Beau pulled her close for a moment and said, "You can come here any time you like."

* * *

GiGi was on the phone when they returned. They could hear her talking and laughing. They were sure she was talking with her sister Ginny. They sounded like a couple of schoolgirls.

Gracie asked, "Can you come in for a bit?"

"I will stay long enough to thank Mrs. Douglas for the goodies and for letting me steal you away," Beau said as he sat down in the double-rocker on the porch. He patted the chair cushion beside him so Gracie would sit down by him. She sat down and he reached for Gracie's hand.

"Maybe I should kiss you goodnight before GiGi

comes back out?" Gracie smiled and he leaned in to kiss her. It was one of those kisses that made her feel lost in time and floating. It was a kiss that she would never forget.

Gracie finally said, "It sounds like they may be on the phone longer than we first thought."

"I should get going or you'll never get me off this porch after that kiss."

Gracie blushed. Beau cupped his hands around Gracie's face, looked in her eyes and said, "Goodnight, Twinkle."

"Goodnight."

As he walked away, Gracie could feel something she hadn't felt since she was last here. She watched his taillights until they were no longer visible. She sighed lightly and went inside to wait for GiGi to end her phone call. As it turned out, GiGi was still on the phone after 10 more minutes. Gracie walked by and GiGi shrugged her shoulders and smiled. Gracie pointed up the stairs, and GiGi threw her a kiss. Gracie headed upstairs, showered, and got ready for bed. As she laid there, she reminisced about the last couple of months and how things had changed in such a positive way. She thanked God for bringing her through it all. After her prayers, she thought of Beau again. Those blue eyes and that killer smile were enough to send her into an unbelievably soft and peaceful slumber.

11

Gracie received the interview call from HR first thing in the morning.

"Hello, Gracie. I am calling to set up your interview. Would you be able to come next Monday at 10 a.m.? You'll be meeting with our HR Director, Ms. Lynn."

"Yes, that would be fine."

"I believe you know your way around here, so we will see you soon."

"Thank you and I look forward to seeing you. Goodbye."

Gracie was so excited; she ran downstairs to tell her grandmother who was sitting out on the porch with her coffee. Gracie poured a quick cup and went outside to give the update.

"Well, what did they say, Girlie?"

"Interview next week after you leave. Can you believe it? I was hoping you could ride along and have lunch with Uncle John."

"We will be long gone by then. I do hope this will be your dream job, and you will want to stay. Have you had any thoughts on other opportunities?"

"Yes, but they were all on the East or West Coast. Max wanted me to come to Europe, but that doesn't really count. Those places were all too far from you and, besides, I have a job housesitting until you get back, ha."

GiGi's belly-laugh always made Gracie laugh more.

"Good decision, Dear! Definitely a win-win for all of us."

* * *

GiGi's ship-off date seemed to come quickly. She had given Gracie specific directions about taking care of the lawn, flower gardens, coy pond, and checking in on her neighbor well in advance of the trip.

"What can I carry to the car for you, GiGi?

"It's all by the door. Thank you, Dear. I am so excited!"

"Keep your distance from the polar bears. I hear they are hungry this time of year. Just kidding! The temps should be milder than they are during the other months."

"True and I will definitely need my sunglasses while in the Land of the Midnight Sun!"

"How wonderful, GiGi! You can do your sightseeing day and night!"

They laughed while entering the car and heading to meet up with Uncle John and Aunt Ginny. GiGi reminded Gracie about her list of things to take care of. Gracie just smiled.

"We're here! I will see you soon, Luv."

"Goodbye all!" Gracie put the top down and waved as she headed back home. She was anxious to get everything prepared for the interview in a few days. She had already planned her wardrobe and the resumes were printed. She thought she might splurge and get a manicure before the event. She wanted to organize her thoughts for the event. It had been a while since she had been through the interview process. She was familiar with the company and layout of the facility. She really didn't feel nervous about the interview, just a little anxious. She really wasn't sure what type of job they might offer her if they offered anything. Time will tell, she thought. God has a plan.

The phone rang and it was Beau. "Have you heard anything regarding an interview?

"Yes, it's coming up in a few days."

"Do you have any plans tonight?"

"Not yet. What's up?"

"There's a concert tonight at the outdoor amphitheater. Warning you, though, Mom and Dad will be there, and we might run into them since it's a small venue."

"I'd love it. Local artists playing?"

"Yes. They're surprisingly good. Pick you up at seven, and we'll eat a bite there too?"

"I'll be ready."

"Well, all righty then."

When Gracie got back to the cottage, she remembered she hadn't eaten anything and decided to raid the fridge. Cinnamon rolls, yes! She walked over and warmed up a cup of leftover coffee from the pot from earlier that morning and headed out to the porch. The activity on the water seemed to be picking up. She watched the sailboats glide by. The water was so clear and not turbulent. She observed the happy faces and listened to the laughter of those who were closer to shore. She was mindful of the danger at sea and couldn't wait to get out there again. She wondered if Beau or any of his friends had a boat. Papa used to have one, but GiGi sold it after a while. She could not bear to go out on the sea without him, and Gracie understood that. She finished her roll and decided to take a walk down the beach. She hoped she would find some sand dollars and star fish.

* * *

Beau picked up Gracie promptly at seven. She was ready and walked down to meet him as he pulled up.

"You ready for a big night in the city?"

"I sure am!"

"Well, let's go. Are you hungry for anything in particular?"

"I would love some fresh crab cakes. What do you think?"

"I know the perfect place," Beau said as he placed his hand on Gracie's.

She absolutely loved it when he did that. She looked out the window at the sky and it looked so billowy. So many shapes that truly looked like any animal you could imagine.

"Here we are," Beau said as he hopped out and opened Gracie's door.

"I am ready for some crab cakes for sure!"

"This way, Madam!"

They walked over to one of the newer outside cafes that Gracie had not been to and waited to be seated. Beau knew everyone there, and Gracie didn't mind. He was so kind and personable. She was sure everyone loved him.

"Can we sit where we can see the water?"

"Of course, Beau. How about here?" the waiter asked.

"Perfect."

Beau smiled and said, "We really don't need a menu. We would just like crab cakes for two with your normal sides. What would you like to drink, Gracie?"

"Whatever you are having," Gracie responded.

Beau finished ordering, and they could see that the amphitheater was starting to get full.

"Do we need to get our food to go?"

Beau said, "No, I have a spot already reserved over there, so don't hurry. Enjoy those crab cakes. I certainly am."

"I think these are the best ever!"

Once they finished, Beau led Gracie over to a spot by a group of palm trees. He had brought a blanket and two chairs for them to sit on. The acoustics were great, and they could see each performer as they played. It was a perfect night under the stars. When the performances were over, Gracie noticed a couple looking at them and talking to each other.

"Beau, do you know that couple?"

"It's my mom and dad. Are you ready to meet them?"

"If you are ready for me to meet them? Gracie answered.

Beau waved them over, and they walked quickly over to them.

"Gracie, we are so glad to meet you. Beau said he had met you a couple of months ago and thought you would be back for the summer. I'm Joel and this is Beau's mother, Callista," Beau's father said.

"It's so nice to meet you both."

"We do hope you will come for dinner this summer once you get settled in. Joel is great on the grill," Callista said.

"I would love that."

"We will look forward to it too. I must tell you that you have a very striking resemblance to your mother, Joy. She was exceptionally beautiful. We both knew her and your father and thought so much of them."

"Oh, thank you very much," Gracie squeaked out.

"We will see you soon. Goodnight."

As they walked away, Beau started gathering the chairs and blanket.

"I hope that wasn't too uncomfortable for you."

"No, it was really okay. They seem genuinely nice."

"Everyone says so," Beau said and laughed. "Were you okay with my mom's comment?"

"Yes, I love it when anyone remembers my parents and says something. You know, it keeps her and my father's memories alive."

"Did you want some dessert or are you ready to head home?"

"I probably should head back. I really don't like to come in late by myself after dark. You wouldn't think I would be such a chicken."

"I get it. I will check the house before I leave if you like?"

"I would really appreciate it, Beau."

"Consider it done."

When they pulled in the drive, Gracie remembered that she didn't leave the porch light on as well as any interior lights.

"I didn't realize how dark it is here without any lights left on."

"It's a good thing I am here to go in first," Beau said and laughed. He turned on his cell phone flashlight so they could see better as they walked in. "And I think GiGi needs a dog."

Beau guided Gracie up the front porch stairs, and she handed him the key.

"Can you sit on the porch for a bit?"

"Yes, after I check the house for you. Deal?"

"Deal! Would you like a cold beverage or will it keep you awake this late?"

"Water is good."

"Water it is." Gracie pulled out a pitcher of water with oranges, lemons, and limes cut up in it, poured two glasses, and waited by the door.

When Beau finished checking everything, he came to the front door, and they went outside.

"Thank you for a wonderful night," Gracie said. "It was nice to meet your parents and not too awfully awkward."

"Now, that's funny! They were probably more nervous than you."

"Well, anyway…"

"And how about those crab cakes, Gracie?"

"Magnificent! We will do that again, and I will buy, ha."

Beau patted the cushion by him for Gracie to come and sit by him. He reached out for her hand, and they just sat and looked at the moon and stars for a bit. No words were needed between them.

"I'm so glad you are home, Twinkle."

Gracie laid her head on Beau's shoulder. She was glad, too.

He leaned down and kissed the top of her head, and Gracie reached up and pulled Beau to her. He put his arms around her, and they both sighed at the same time, then began to laugh.

They both wondered if this could be real.

"Who would have thought that after meeting a few months ago, we would be sitting here together at this time like this?" Beau asked.

"I don't know, Beau, but here we are," Gracie quickly replied.

"A divine meeting then?"

"I do believe so, too."

12

Monday seemed to arrive quickly and as Gracie was preparing for her interview, she pondered on the past weekend. One of the weekend highlights was that Beau had invited her to church on the beach. It was vastly different from anything she had experienced before and was immensely powerful. Beau was friends with the couple who were missionaries and were in the U.S. for a month to visit their family. He said he had gone to high school with them. While they were here, they decided to offer church services Sunday morning and evening on the beach. Beau said the attendance grew with each service. There were three decisions made to accept Christ and two rededications the morning that Gracie attended. It was amazing.

Gracie hurried to get ready for her first interview as a college graduate. She was excited to think that she might be employed soon. What an impressive thought! Once ready, she grabbed her bag and a cup of coffee for the short commute and said a quick prayer before leaving the driveway.

* * *

Gracie's interview and lunch went well. She was very hopeful after leaving. They were very cordial and hospitable and told her they would be in touch by Friday as they were still in the interview process. Gracie thanked them and headed back toward the cottage. As she was leaving the parking garage, she noticed a sign for a botanical garden and aquarium. She wondered if that was something new of if she had been too busy to ever notice it before. That would be something she could offer when her friends came to visit. With that thought, she decided to give Julie a call to see when she could come for a visit. Julie answered her phone when she called.

"Hey, Julie, I can't believe you actually picked up!"

Julie laughed and said, "What's up?"

"When do you think you can come for a visit?"

"Any time that works for you!"

"You're not employed yet either?" Gracie asked.

"Not yet, but I had an interview last week in your state!"

"That's great. You can tell me all about your job offer and location when you get here. Do you think we should schedule quickly in case one or both of us get job offers since we may have to be adulting soon?

"Yes, for sure!"

"When can you get here?"

"How about Wednesday? I've got to take care of some things here for my family before I can come."

"Great! I'll see you then. You remember how to get here, right?"

"I sure do. See you Wednesday. Bye!"

"Bye, Julie!"

* * *

Gracie received a text message from Beau a little

while later, asking how everything went.

She stopped and texted back, "Can you come for dinner tonight at six p.m. and we'll talk all about it? You do like other seafood besides crab cakes, right?"

Beau texted back, "Yes, I love it all. I'll be there."

Gracie text back and replied with a smiley face.

Now she had to figure out what she would fix Beau for dinner. A shrimp boil for two might be good, she thought. If it turned out well, she might make it again when Julie was here for her visit. Good practice, she thought. GiGi is the chef in our family, but I have learned quite a bit from her.

Gracie thought she would stop by the Seaside Market to pick up a few items she needed once she was back to town. She thought about items needed for the boil: fresh shrimp, corn on the cob, small red potatoes, kielbasa, garlic, onion, and all the spices. She thought she had everything except for the fresh shrimp.

When she arrived, she ran in to pick up the shrimp. She was disappointed that Beau was not there, but Gracie was incredibly happy with all the fresh seafood that they had. She thought she might throw a few clams in there as well.

She did not feel that an appetizer was necessary with that much food. She thought she would make garlic rolls and strawberry pretzel dessert cups. She would make a citrus punch with plenty of sliced oranges, limes and lemons served in jelly jars. All items were easy to prepare and wouldn't take her whole afternoon to prep.

Gracie hurried in with her items, changed out of her suit and heels, and happily began getting everything ready for dinner.

At about five-thirty, Beau popped in.

"I'm a little early. I thought I could help some."

"Your timing is perfect! All ingredients are ready once the water is boiling. Do you mind turning on the propane cooker outside to get it started?"

"I can do that!"

Beau headed outside to the pergola and turned on the cooker.

The water began to boil, and Gracie tossed in the larger items. She didn't add the shrimp until everything else was prepared and ready.

"This looks great! I can't wait to dig in."

"Grab that ladle if you don't mind and we'll scoop it all in that large round crock sitting on the table. Once in the crock, please add the butter sitting there on the side table, and I'll grab the salad and drinks."

"Got it!" Beau did his best not to spill or drop any of the food. "I may need a bib once we start eating."

"Me too," Gracie laughed. "Let's sit out here to eat."

"Good plan! This is so good, Gracie. Thanks for going to all the trouble to fix this tonight. Now tell me all about your interview."

Gracie shared all about the interview and how they had contract work as well as full time work there.

"The benefit of the contract work is that it will allow me to "tryout" the job on a limited basis and work from home at my own pace. The benefit of full time is just that it is full time with full time benefits."

"Is pay a consideration between the two possible

offers?"

"The contract work would pay a little more because it has no benefits. I prefer the contract work first to see how it goes. I really like the idea of no commuting or relocation."

"I hope you get what your heart desires, Gracie."

"If you only knew," Gracie thought.

"Yes, me, too, Beau. Are you ready for strawberry pretzel cups?

"I sure am. Can I help you? What about a little more to drink? I love the fresh fruit in the drinks." This drink was perfect for the surprise that Beau had planned for Gracie.

"What do you say we take our dessert and eat it down on Water's Edge Lane?

"Yes, let's go!"

"Gracie, you can drive."

"You want me to cook and drive?"

"Yes, I do this time." Beau was smiling ear to ear.

"Are you up to something, Beau?"

Beau just continued smiling, answered, and handed Gracie the keys, "We'd better get going!"

Once they arrived, Beau asked Gracie to wait a couple minutes while he pulled a couple of things together.

As Gracie walked up the path slowly, Beau called out, "I have a small graduation gift for you. It seems really appropriate after our dinner beverages."

Gracie hurried over to see three miniature fruit trees. There was a lemon tree, a lime tree, and an orange tree.

"These are for me?"

"They sure are. You can keep them in the pots until you find your permanent place.

"I love these, Beau."

"I thought you might! With that comment, Beau scooped Gracie up in his arms and spun around.

"What do you say we finish our desserts and take a little hike over to that building over there?"

Gracie turned around to look at the area where Beau was pointing.

"What's over there?"

"You'll see. Come on."

Beau reached out his hand, then pulled Gracie on his back to piggy-back her over to the building. Gracie wrapped her arms around Beau. He giggled and that made Gracie giggle more. Beau opened the door. Inside was a sailboat!

"I didn't know you had a sailboat!"

"Our family has had other types of boats through the years, but I wanted to buy my own. I began looking for one right after I bought this land here. It sure did not take me long to find the right one.

Beau gave Gracie a high-five, and they begin checking the boat and sails over to ensure everything was in place.

"What's her name?" Gracie asked.

"Since she is brand new, I haven't named her yet. Help me decide, Gracie. You know there's an old superstition that it's bad luck not to name your boat."

"Well, we can't leave tonight until we have a name. Okay, how about Crosswinds?

"Keep going with that thought."

"Water's Edge?"

"I'm liking that. Anything else in your repertoire?"

"Beau, do you like S.S. Souvenir?"

"That's it! Third time is a charm."

"When can we christen her?" Isn't that proper boating etiquette? Gracie inquired. "How about on your birthday?"

"What? How did you know my birthday is coming up?"

"A little shore birdie told me. Beau, we share birthdays, but that's our secret with the little birdie."

"There you go again, Gracie. You totally amaze me every day. That little birdie didn't happen to be GiGi, was it?"

Gracie put her hand on her lips as if she were locking them up, the way GiGi does sometimes, then smiled and gave Beau a quick side hug. At that point, he pulled her back and held on to her a little longer.

"Beau, for your birthday, I would like to add the name to the boat for you. I really can't surprise you with that since it's your boat." Gracie made a funny face and rolled her eyes, and Beau burst out laughing.

"You're right. That would be great. Thank you, Gracie. I'll get it scheduled at the marina, and we'll make a day of it maybe this weekend?"

"The following weekend might be better. Remember, Julie is coming in a few days and staying through the weekend. Hey, do you think we could get the bicycle group together like you did when I first met everyone and spend the evening at the pier?"

"Sure!" Beau quickly answered.

"She loved it when I told her how I met everyone."

"Which reminds me, and I almost forgot."

"Reminds you of what?"

"My parents are having a birthday bash for me next Sunday at the house. I hope you aren't too busy."

"Of course, I am not too busy. Can I help your mom with anything?"

"I think she has it covered. All we need is you to be there. I'll give you all the details when I know them, ha."

"Beau, I do have one problem though."

"What is that?"

"How am I going to bring the ship to the party so they can see what I got you?"

Beau burst out laughing. "Oh, believe me, they'll know. I'll see if they can get the boat in earlier so it's ready by party time."

"I'll tell Julie to bring her party dress, so she can stop in on her way out of town."

"No party dress needed. It will be casual."

"Maybe a sundress then," Gracie cocked her head and winked.

"Maybe so."

"Gracie, it's getting dark, and the sun is setting. Let's head over to the chairs and chill. Grab a couple of beverages out of the fridge for us."

Gracie grabbed the drinks and followed Beau back to the small pier. The sun was beginning to set, and colors were so vivid. Gracie could not tell where the orange, magenta, gold, and purple colors started and stopped. They all blended so beautifully.

"Here you go, Captain!"

"Have a seat, Matey!"

"Aye, aye, Captain."

"You are hilarious, Gracie."

Instead of sitting in the chair, Gracie sat down on the warm wooden planks to dangle her feet in the water. She could see the marine life below and was so focused on the fish, she didn't notice that Beau stood up and took his shirt off until she heard this large splash on the other side of the pier.

"Come on in. The water's great!"

Gracie backed up and ran to make a huge cannonball splash right next to Beau.

"What do you think about that, Captain?"

"I think you are pretty special. Now come here. The captain is responsible for his crew, and it's kind of deep on this side."

Gracie swam over to Beau. He held her in the water for a bit, then turned her around to give her a big kiss.

"Last one to the pier has to swab the deck," Beau commanded.

Gracie pushed Beau backward and swam as fast as she could.

"Hmmm, guess you'll be swabbing the deck tonight, Captain."

Beau threw his keys to Gracie and said, "All right, you get to drive home then."

Once they arrived, Beau walked Gracie to the door and asked, "Do you want me to check things out before I leave?"

"Would you mind?"

"I'm on it." Beau went about the house while Gracie changed into dry clothes. She grabbed her jacket since the wind had picked up.

"I'll be on the porch with more drinks."

Beau sure liked the sound of that. He loved how everything was homemade at their house and how most of the furniture and paintings were made by family and had stayed in the family for years.

"As Beau came out the door, he asked, "Gracie, I noticed a book of poetry upstairs. Would I be able to read it sometime?"

"It was Grandma Sophie's poetry. You can read it, but you will have to read it here. GiGi wouldn't want that book leaving this property without proper security."

Beau shook his head and laughed.

Gracie patted the chair cushion the way Beau usually did. He walked over to her and stopped. "I am soaked. Are you sure you want me to sit there?"

"Let me grab one of Papa's work shirts for you to put on. It's getting a little chilly."

Beau followed Gracie inside. As she handed Beau the shirt, Beau grabbed Gracie's jacket collar, pulled her close, and said, "I'm so glad you are here." He then kissed her the same gentle way he did the last time. Again, she felt is if she were floating. Gracie took Beau's hand and led him back to the front porch. This time he pulled Gracie on his lap and put his arms around her.

To Gracie it seemed that this was so comfortable and like they had always done this. To Beau, it felt like home.

"I'm not letting you go, Gracie."

"Promise?"

"I promise."

13

Gracie slept in since Julie would be arriving on Wednesday afternoon. She knew that they would be up extremely late Wednesday night talking and sharing about everything going on in their lives. As she was getting ready to make some coffee, the phone rang. It was the HR Dept.

They called to offer her a contract position with the option of becoming full-time at the end of the contract. The pay was more than she had expected. They told her they would email the paperwork for her to review and return by next Monday. Gracie immediately texted Beau to tell him. He replied instantly and told her how proud he was of her.

Gracie had a new hop to her step as she started some light cleaning and laundry while the morning coffee was brewing. The aroma filled the air, and it reminded her of mornings with GiGi on the porch.

Gracie received a text from Julie saying, that she should arrive by six p.m. tonight. She had a few unexpected things come up and she would explain later. Gracie hoped everything was okay for her dear friend. She thought about all the things they could do during Julie's visit. There was the beach and then there was the beach. There was no question that they would enjoy the beach all week! Gracie thought she might surprise her with the aquarium and botanical gardens.

As Gracie was tidying up, she wondered how GiGi's group was doing. She viewed the trip itinerary and saw that they should arrive in Juneau for the week. Gracie knew they were having the time of their lives and hoped to hear from them soon. She knew HR would contact Uncle John to tell him that she had verbally accepted the position. She was so thankful and said a quick prayer of thanksgiving for her job, her family, friends, and for Beau.

Next, she thought she would prepare the guest room for Julie. She grabbed clean sheets and pillowcases, cleaning items, and went to work. She even placed fresh flowers from GiGi's Garden on the nightstand by the bed. Lastly, she finished off the room with candy from the local seaside candy store in antique glassware from the cupboard.

Once everything was clean and ready, Gracie decided to take her daily stroll along the beach. She found several larger seashells and placed them in the bottom of her t-shirt as she walked along the water's edge. She loved observing the little children running back and forth with the tide coming in and going out, families playing in the sand making sandcastles, but the thing she loved most was the happy faces all along the beach.

***

Julie arrived right on time at six p.m., and Gracie was already grilling steaks for dinner for them.

"I'm so glad to finally be here!"

"Let me help you get your things to the

guestroom. It's right off the dining room. I thought you would prefer an ocean-view room, ha! Am I wrong?"

"You are right on! Any room is okay with me. I could sleep on the porch or patio and would be fine with that, too."

"Go ahead and get settled and I will have dinner ready in about fifteen minutes. There are towels and washcloths in the bathroom if you would like to take a quick shower or freshen up."

Gracie finished the twice-baked potatoes and salad. The table was already set up outside. Gracie hollered, "I fixed steaks tonight because we will probably be eating seafood the rest of the week. Sound good?"

"Yes, I can't wait to dig in!"

As Julie came out the French doors, she said, "Bird of Paradise and fresh-made candy by my bed? Wow!"

"Nothing but the best for my bestie."

The girls began eating and caught up with everything that was going on in their lives currently. Julie shared that she had three interviews coming up in the next few weeks. Gracie shared about her job offer.

"We will celebrate both of our new jobs when your interviewing is complete. What do you say?" Gracie asked. "Maybe another week here on the beach before you start? Do you think they will want you to start immediately, or will you have some time?"

"I'm sure I will have to relocate wherever I end up, so they should give me time for that. I am not planning to actually move much furniture and hope to find a furnished apartment."

"Great, then I hope that means you'll be back?"

"With bells on!" Julie whispered.

Both began to laugh and plan out their week, starting with the Botanical Gardens tomorrow, Aquarium on her last day, and lots of beach time in between. Gracie mentioned the Bicycle Club and the friends she had met.

"Would you like to ride with the group while you are here?"

"I would love it. I need some exercise if we keep eating like this." Julie puffed out her cheeks as if she was going to explode, and they chuckled.

"It's a good thing then, because they will be riding by in about an hour to check to see if we are ready. I think you will really like everyone."

"Can't wait then."

After dinner, the girls placed the dishes in the sink and went out on the porch to wait for the group to ride up. While waiting, Gracie shared her last day with Max and all that occurred. Julie was empathetic and thankful that she had shared what she had seen with Gracie. Otherwise, Gracie may have had a life with someone that did not deserve her. Gracie was such a kind, loving, and gentle soul.

***

The group rode up and Beau was leading the pack. She could see his blue eyes from a distance.

Julie asked, "Is that Beau in front of the group?"

Gracie nodded her head and smiled.

"Well, I can see what is keeping you here much

better now."

The girls began to cackle. They hurried down to meet the group on their bikes. Gracie introduced Julie to everyone, and they welcomed Julie, much the same way that they did Gracie. She was so glad.

"Where are we riding tonight? Gracie asked.

"As if you didn't know!" Beau said.

When they reached the pier, a couple of the guys were already there with a fire going. It smelled like they were making S'mores.

"Come and get your S'mores! Hot off the fire!" they roared.

The group sat around the fire and shared what their summers held for them. Julie was glad to be a part of it all. Gracie noticed that one of the guys in the group had caught Julie's eye, but Gracie did not say anything about it. His name was Liam.

"Is everyone ready to head back now? It's 10 o'clock, and I turn into a pumpkin soon," Beau asked.

Everyone agreed and put out the fire.

"Will we see you two tomorrow night? Beau asked.

"You can count on it."

After the girls returned home, Julie stopped Gracie as they were walking into the cottage and said, "I understand why you came back."

Gracie beamed and said, "I can't imagine being anywhere else."

14

The girls had a fun week together enjoying the sun, sand, and beach. Julie appreciated their trip to the aquarium and botanical gardens. They both agreed the gardens would be a beautiful place for a wedding.

Gracie was a little preoccupied thinking of Beau's birthday party later today. "I have no idea what to wear. What do you think, maybe a sundress?"

Julie replied, "If it's outside, a sundress would be perfect. "Happy birthday to you too. I brought you a gift. Here you go."

Gracie slowly opened the gift. It was a beautiful silver cross necklace. "I love this, Julie! Help me put it on."

Julie gladly assisted Gracie with the clasp. "It's perfect."

The phone began to ring for a FaceTime call. GiGi, Uncle John, and Aunt Ginny began singing Happy Birthday in perfect harmony.

"You all need to take this show on the road!"

"We are hoping your birthday is going well, Luv. We wish we could be there to celebrate with you. We are glad Julie is there though! Congratulations on your job offer, too!"

Yes, that was a wonderful birthday present, and I am extremely excited about it."

Gracie could hear the ship captain calling "All aboard" in the background.

"I love and miss you all. Have fun! Goodbye."

Gracie had noticed that Julie had disappeared during the call.

"Here's your cake, Gracie! There's ice cream in the freezer."

"Now, how did you maneuver all of this?"

Julie quickly answered, "I had a little help from some friends. Ready to dig in?" She placed a small candle on the cake. "Now make a wish and blow it out."

Gracie did as she directed and wished that today would be one of the best days of her life. She didn't think that anything could be any better than this. Her favorite chocolate sheet cake, her best friend, and an evening celebrating Beau's birthday.

* * *

Gracie and Julie left in plenty of time to follow Beau's directions to his parents' home for the party. Gracie, still a little nervous, told Julie how she had paid for the name to be added to Beau's new sailboat.

"That's when you come back, we should be able to take you out then. When you get your sea legs."

"Yes!"

As they neared the property, there were exceptionally large and old magnolia trees that were blooming all the way up the drive. Once inside the front gate, palm trees and many flowering trees and bushes were all lining the property. Gracie had no idea that Beau's family had such a large estate.

"These blooming magnolias are almost better

than the six-hundred-year-old tree that still stands in St. Augustine."

"I'd love to see that someday," Julie said. "What kind of tree is it?"

"It's a live oak tree, and it was named Old Senator. It's near the Fountain of Youth!"

"Very funny!"

"At least it's in the same town!"

Julie shook her head and said, "We're going to have to go on a road trip when I'm back again."

"You can count on it."

As they arrived near the doorway, Beau came out to direct them as a New York police officer would direct traffic. Gracie thought that he looked more handsome than ever.

"He always takes my breath away."

Julie agreed, "I can see that."

"Glad you are here a little early, so you can choose your favorite table out on the patio. Save me a spot at your table, okay? You remember Liam, don't you?"

Julie answered quickly. "I do."

Gracie looked at Beau, and they both laughed.

"I thought you might, Julie. He remembered you too. I've got to get busy helping Mom. Make yourselves at home. Drinks and hors d'oeuvres are set up before dinner. I hope you're excited about more seafood, girls! Take a walk around the grounds. My place is over there above the garage. You can go in if you like."

Gracie looked over at the five-car-garage and thought his place must be about three times the size of

GiGi's cottage.

"You can call out to Romeo from the exterior staircase," Julie mused.

Gracie agreed with the nod of her head. She glanced back to the house and Beau's parents were busily welcoming their guests. Gracie had no idea who all these people were.

"We'd better head that way," Gracie said. "Here come the butterflies."

"Butterflies as in people or your stomach?"

"Stomach," Gracie replied flatly.

As they sat down, Liam headed their way.

"Don't look now, but here comes Liam."

"I feel the butterflies now," Julie whispered.

"Hello, Gracie! Hi, Julie. I'm not sure if you remember me, but I'm Liam."

"Yes, I remember you," Julie said.

"Thanks for sitting with us. You wouldn't mind sharing who are friends and who are family?" Gracie asked.

"Anything to help out." Liam bowed and said, "At your service, ladies. Now what can I get you to drink?" Liam asked.

"Maybe Julie can assist you carrying the food?" Gracie asked.

"Perfect!"

As Gracie watched them walk away, she could see that they were getting along greatly, laughing, and talking. It was such a beautiful night. She could see Beau walking around, owning the room with ease. He saw her sitting alone and came directly over to her.

"Why don't you come and walk around with me so I can show you off?" Beau asked.

"I will, but only because it's your birthday," Gracie added.

"It's our birthday. Happy birthday, Twinkle."

Gracie pulled Beau down so she could whisper, "Happy birthday, Beau."

Beau made sure that he introduced Gracie to everyone at the party. Most of the people that she met knew GiGi and asked about her. Gracie could tell that GiGi was well thought of here in this town.

Beau's father announced, "Before we honor the birthday boy, I would like to make an important announcement. Beau recently graduated from college, and we are happy to announce that he has accepted a position at our accounting firm and will begin the new position next month. "Everyone began clapping and whistling. Beau looked over at Gracie because he hadn't told her yet. She gave him a thumbs up sign. Gracie snapped a quick picture of Beau.

"Now let's get back to our original business. It's time for cake, birthday wishes, and a song, everyone! Let's sing!"

Everyone began to sing. Beau made a wish and snuffed out the candle, then looked up at Gracie. Out of nowhere, Beau's mother came out carrying another cake with a sparkler on it and announced, "We have two birthdays today, so please join us in wishing Gracie a happy birthday too."

In perfect timing, everyone said, "Happy birthday, Gracie!" Beau chimed in and sang in a minor tone, "And many more!"

Gracie was in shock. "Thank you all. I really am surprised!"

Everyone clapped as Beau's parents began cutting the cakes. Beau leaned in to give Gracie a side hug.

Gracie asked, "Is this the best night ever or what?"

"See those palm trees over there by the water?" Beau asked. Gracie nodded. "I'll meet you there after everyone leaves tonight, okay?"

"Sure." Gracie wondered what he had in mind.

"Beau, Julie will have to be leaving soon to get on the road, so I will walk her out to her car when she's ready."

"Maybe Liam will walk with you!" Beau said with a big grin.

Gracie walked over to see what time Julie was planning to leave.

"The band is getting ready to start to play and they just happened to be playing my favorite song. She has to stay for at least one dance," Liam insisted.

"What do you say, Julie?" Gracie asked.

"I can stay for one dance."

Liam smiled as he pulled Julie out on the dance floor. The song happened to be a slow one to dance to. Beau came up behind Gracie and pulled her to the dance floor as well. Both couples seemed to glide around the dance floor and many other couples joined them. Beau pulled Gracie close to him and said, "I could definitely get used to this." Gracie nodded in agreement.

When the song was over, Liam asked to walk

with them to the car. Liam asked Julie if she had a pen. She reached in her purse and handed it to him. He wrote his number on her hand and asked her to call him when she arrived home so he wouldn't worry about her. She gladly agreed.

"Beau, I will be back shortly. I don't want Julie driving on the road too late."

"Not to add any pressure or anything, but she could stay in town another night and leave early tomorrow morning with plenty of sunlight?" Liam questioned. "What do you think?"

"I think that would be fine. There would definitely be more daylight."

The couples separated as they walked back toward the party. Gracie was glad that Julie was having an enjoyable time.

"While they were gone, a group of men had pulled the sailboat out to show everyone Beau's new boat with her new name. Beau stepped up and said, "We will christen her soon as the S.S. Souvenir and hope you all join us when we do. The name was Gracie's idea and I think it's very fitting." Everyone clapped and began talking about their boats.

The music began to play again, and they announced that this would be their last song for the night. Beau pulled Gracie back out on the floor and put his arms around her waist. Both closed their eyes as they whirled around on the dance floor. They did not notice Beau's parents watching them dance. When the song was over, Beau said, "Meet me at the three palm trees in five minutes." Gracie agreed.

When they got over there out of everyone's sight, Beau leaned in and cupped his hands on the edges of Gracie's face and said, "Gracie, I know we haven't known each other very long, but being with you feels like home. I want to promise you if we are still together this time next year on our birthdays, I want our party to be an engagement party, and I want to propose on this same spot."

Gracie's eyes widened. She was stunned.

"Is that a yes, no, or I need to think about it?"

"It's definitely yes. I feel the same way, Beau."

They embraced, and Beau kissed her the way he always did which seemed to be in slow motion. She couldn't tell where her lips ended, and his lips started.

"Can we finish this conversation after the party then? This will be our secret, Twinkle." Gracie nodded and was still whirling from what just happened.

"Well, come on then." Beau took Gracie by the hand and led her back to the party. Julie and Liam were sitting at their table.

"We thought you two took off," Liam said with a huge smile.

Julie said, "We can help clean up, Beau."

"No, Liam already told me he would help. We might stop by later if you will still be up and open to company?"

"Perfect!" Gracie answered.

* * *

The girls said their goodbyes and thanked Beau's parents for the wonderful evening. Beau's mother quietly said to Gracie so only she could hear," Beau has never brought anyone home before." Gracie's surprise was very evident.

"What a week!" Gracie said as she circled around back to the cottage.

"Did you have an enjoyable time tonight, Julie?" Julie was deep in her thoughts about her evening with Liam.

"It was better than I ever expected. I am glad the guys are stopping by tonight for a bit. I guess we can offer them more birthday cake and ice cream."

"They are probably still hungry. Just kidding!" Gracie said.

The warm, salty breezes filtered through their hair as Gracie put the top down. There seemed to be more stars than usual. Julie called out the constellations that she had memorized from her recent astronomy class. Gracie was impressed.

"It would be fun for you and Beau to have a contest to see who knows the most constellations."

"Sounds like fun. Tonight?"

"Sure, you want to make the challenge, Julie?"

"Yes, of course. You know I'll win," Julie said and pointed up to the sky. "There's Orion up there winking at us, but that's an easy one."

"This should be fun! Since you must get up early, maybe we should see how many can be named in ten minutes by each team?"

"Well, I have a slight advantage, since I already know about the challenge."

"That's true. Let's just search them out together on the porch tonight."

Gracie received a text from Beau stating that they would not be able to stop by as he and Liam needed to help a couple guests get their vehicles home. He mentioned he would text Gracie later to say goodnight. Beau said that Liam was disappointed and hoped that Julie would text him when she arrived home tomorrow.

Gracie shared the update from Beau with Julie. "Unfortunately, I guess we will have to save the constellation challenge for next time. We'd better head to bed. What time are you leaving in the morning?"

Julie said, "I'd like to be on the road by daylight."

"Homemade cinnamon rolls and coffee sound good for breakfast?" Gracie asked.

"Sounds great! See you in the morning, Gracie."

"Goodnight."

Gracie turned off the lights and headed up the stairs to bed. She pondered about Julie's visit, the week, and today. Gracie hoped that Julie would come back soon.

Suddenly, Gracie felt very tired and climbed into bed. As she laid there, she smiled and thought of Beau's gentle caress and unexpected promise by the three palm trees. Somehow, she knew they would be there next year celebrating an engagement along with their birthdays.

Again, she thought about God and how He had been so good to her.

15

The girls awoke early. Julie packed her car while Gracie fixed cinnamon rolls. When all the packing was done and coffee ready, Gracie asked, "Breakfast in the Secret Garden or on the porch?"

"Secret Garden has my vote."

Gracie nodded and carried the breakfast tray out to the garden area.

"This is great. We were so busy; we didn't get to spend any time out here in the Secret Garden. I remember playing dress up with you out here and those tea parties!"

"Those were the days, Julie. We did have some fun."

"Remember how your mom and grandma would dress up with us and your grandpa would act like our butler?"

"I sure do. We were so blessed, weren't we?"

"Just think what we would have done if the coy pond had been there, Gracie!"

"We probably would have become mermaids, and my mom would definitely have joined in! See those shells by the pond? GiGi told me that when my mom was a little girl, she would use the conch shells for telephones to call the mermaids."

"We definitely could have played along with that!

I see lots of mermaid items for kids in the stores, and I always think of you, Gracie. With those sweet memories, I had better get on the road."

The girls walked through the house and out on the porch. "Now Julie, tell me when you're coming back?"

"As soon as I know the result of my interviews. Hey, look who's riding up the bike path!" Julie said with a huge smile. "Hi, guys! In the neighborhood?"

"We just happen to be heading your way. Somebody wanted to say good-bye. He also wanted to ensure that his number didn't wash off your hand." Beau turned his head directly to look at Liam.

"Yes, all is true. Here is my card, just in case the number faded." Liam handed Julie his card.

"Liam Smith, Director of Marketing, Seaview County Hospital. Is this a new job for you?"

"Yes, I start next week. I completed my internship there and volunteered all through high school and college. It's a great place. You all will have to stop by on your next visit, and I'll give you the grand tour. We also have that name-brand coffee there that everyone loves. I wrote my personal cell number on the back, Julie."

"Got it, thank you. I will text you when I get home. You, too, Julie." They all began to laugh.

"Bring it in for a group hug. You know how I am about taking pics. Now everyone say 'cheese'!"

* * *

Soon after everyone left, Gracie checked her email to ensure that everything was received for her job offer. The letter stated that her start date would be July 1st, and she would begin with new employee orientation for about a week with holiday pay on the Fourth of July. The salary was perfect, allowing her enough money to live on her own or buy a new car if she chose to. Of course, she didn't want to do either. With no college debt, she had a great start in her new profession. She thought she might pay GiGi for rent and groceries if GiGi would let her stay here. Gracie wanted to spend as much time with her as she could with GiGi being seventy years old. She wanted to cook, travel, and spend time helping her in the garden. They were such a good team.

With her job starting soon, Gracie thought she should carefully plan her last free week. She thought of all the places she had always wanted to visit and pondered on who might be able to travel with her. Her international dream trip would be to go to Greece and stay on the Island of Crete.

An in-country one-week trip would be traveling to:

Day one - San Antonio
Day two - cross the border into Mexico
Day three - Sonoma, Arizona
Day four - Lake Tahoe
Day five – Yellowstone
Day six – Seattle
Day seven – Colorado
Home

Realistically, that is more of a three-week plan and some day she will be able to do it. For now, she needed to take care of GiGi's home and chill out before the real work started. Working from home would be perfect for her. She thought she would try to set up her own home office in the spare bedroom downstairs since there was a desk already there. It also has a door for privacy while working. She thought she would buy a temporary storage bin for her office supplies. This way, she can roll it into the closet when not in use. Her new company should offer her all the office supplies needed such as a laptop, printer, paper, and all other items needed, but she thought she would go ahead and make of list of needed items for her first day.

Gracie was very enthusiastic getting everything ready. There was one thing that she absolutely had to have for her new home office, and she could get that from GiGi's garden.

* * *

Beau texted Gracie that he would be busy getting oriented to his father's company for the next two weeks. He had worked there before to help when needed, but in a different role. Gracie was glad in a way. It would give her some time to get prepared for her new job. Beau thought he might stop by with pizza tonight after work if she didn't mind. She was glad that he was coming. She thought it would be a suitable time to look for a congratulations gift for him online before he got there. After seeing his home, she thought he didn't need much. She wondered if a nice name plate with a business card holder and two pens might be nice for his desk. She thought he said he would have an office and would be working some remotely too.

Julie called to tell Gracie that she made it home, and she was tired from the drive.

"Ok, who did you call first? Liam or me? I don't think you really need to answer that question," Gracie said.

"I can't believe how he wants to stay connected with me. I really am not that good of a dancer!" This made Gracie burst out laughing which in turn made Julie laugh too. "He's already asking when I'm coming back, which I don't mind at all. I just wish I knew!"

"Do keep in touch and best of luck in your upcoming interviews." Gracie could hear Beau pulling up in the drive. "I think Beau just arrived. I will tell him hello for you."

"Please do. Thank you and goodbye for now!"

***

"Pizza delivery for a Ms. Twinkle! Anyone home?" Beau hollered as he walked up on the porch.

"You are early, so you will get an extra tip!" Gracie said quietly.

"I will get a tip?"

"Here's your tip." Gracie smiled. "It's poor manners to walk in a house without knocking first."

"Oh really?" Beau reached out and caught Gracie's arm and pulled her in close. "What do you have to say about this?" He kissed her on the cheek.

"I'd rate it about a four," Gracie teased.

"Well, I can do better than that! Come here, you." He leaned Gracie backward over his arm and gave her the sweetest kiss. Will that do, Ms. Twinkle?"

"Maybe a seven and a half now."

"I can do better. Come with me to my chariot, Souvenir, and I will take you away and we will live happily ever after. What do you have to say about that?"

"It's too early to tell, Good Sir."

Beau picked Gracie and the pizza up with one sweep, carried them both to the Jeep, laughing all the way, and headed toward Water's Edge Lane.

"Here we are! Spinach and artichoke pizza coming right up." Beau handed Gracie two pizza slices.

"Let me get yours for you."

"I've got it. When we're done, we can relax and watch the sun set tonight together. We've missed a few nights, haven't we?"

"Seems so. You know, we're going to have to haul some white powder sand here someday, so we can lie down, watch the sun setting, then count the stars," Gracie said with a smile.

"You're always thinking, aren't you, Twinkle? Counting the stars might take all night."

"I know."

Beau immediately moved closer to sit by Gracie on the pier. "I like the way you think, Twinkle. We will need a telescope, too?"

"That's it," Gracie thought. *"I will get him a telescope!"*

"Beau, what kind of fish are those down there?"

"We have all kinds here. Let me see." Beau jumped down in the water. "Jump in and maybe we'll see manatees."

Gracie jumped in and swam to Beau and replied, "This water is so clear and warm."

"And private! Come here, you," Beau said as he wrapped his arms around Gracie.

16

Gracie was glad to have a Saturday morning to herself. She grabbed her coffee and headed out to the Secret Garden. With June passing so quickly and so much to be thankful for, Gracie soon realized that GiGi would be home soon. She enjoyed getting GiGi's 'picture of the day.' Gracie thought she could go online and order a book of memories for all three of them as a welcome home gift. Gracie knew it would be a trip that they all would remember.

While online, she decided to order Beau's telescope. She found a vintage telescope like the ones on the pier. She thought that would be perfect for Beau's property down Water's Edge Lane if the price were right. She did find one that wasn't too high and ordered it quickly. *"We'll see what Beau thinks of this,"* she thought, smiling to herself. She wanted to get him something original that he would always keep and love.

Gracie started to ponder about her job and how well it was going. She loved working in the bunny slippers that Beau had bought her for her new job working from a home office. The work was challenging, and she loved managing her own schedule. She wondered how it would all work out once GiGi returned.

She decided to move to the front porch. Tourists

were beginning to roll in with the upcoming 4th of July holiday. She realized she had better get her walk in before the beach was too crowded. She slipped back inside, changed her shoes, and headed down the beach. As she was heading down the path, she received a text from Julie.

"Hey there! Is the offer still open to come for the 4th of July weekend? I have lots to share about my new job! I do not officially begin until August 1st with more details to follow."

Gracie immediately texted back, "How soon can you be here?"

Julie responded with a telephone call this time. "Hi again! I can be there tonight or tomorrow, whatever is better for you!"

Gracie replied, "Tonight is great! Come on down! Do you want us to let Liam know that you will be here for the weekend?"

"It was his idea!"

"Great! We will see you soon. Drive safely!"

Gracie hurried to get her walk in and thought this would be the calm before the storm and chuckled to herself. The flags on the beach were green today. The water was calm and so peaceful. The smiles that she encountered down the beach were sweet reminders of her days on the beach with Mama. Mama could build the best sandcastles. She always had a moat around the castle with a drawbridge that was impressive by any sandcastle artist's scale.

Gracie quickly switched gears and decided to send out a group text to Julie, Liam, and Beau. "I will be preparing the renowned and exclusive local dinner favorite, Sophie's Special, if anyone is hungry around seven p.m. tonight. Dress is casual. Hope to see you then! Bring your own beverage of choice."

Immediately, all three returned text messages confirming that they would be there. Gracie thought she should get back home promptly to ensure she had all the ingredients for the Special and for dessert as well. When she arrived back at the cottage, there was a package on the porch with her name on it and a note,

"Dear Twinkle,
This is your late birthday present. I hope you like it.
Always, Beau."

Gracie quickly opened the beautifully wrapped package. Inside was a beautiful star necklace with a diamond in the center of the star. There was also another note attached that read,

"Remember our promise.
Love, Beau"

Gracie grabbed her heart and felt that strange feeling again. She felt as if she were in a dream, and she did not want to wake up.

* * *

Everyone surprisingly arrived on time. The food was ready, and the beverages were cold. Gracie had taken the food out to the Garden area so they could spread out more. Everyone shared about their new jobs and how it was going for them. All were so grateful.

"This was your Grandma Sophie's recipe, right?" Beau asked. "I love it." Julie and Liam agreed. "I already have the hole dug and flat beach rocks ready for the 4th of July clambake. The lobster, corn, clams, mussels, chorizo, and potatoes will be picked up the day before, so if you ladies can make salad, I think we will be all set."

"We'll each make one. Okay, Gracie?" Julie asked. Gracie concurred. "Where are we having the clambake?"

"Down Water's Edge Lane," Beau replied. It's a little more private there. Be sure to bring your swimsuits if you want to swim. It should be fun."

Gracie thought of the last time she and Beau were there in the water and smiled.

"What are you thinking about, Gracie?" Julie asked.

Gracie was quiet.

"Oh, I see!" Liam responded before Gracie could say anything.

"Well, I definitely can't say anything now, ha. Anyone for a sunset walk on the beach? I'll clean up when we get back."

"Let's get going," Liam said.

* * *

Once the group started walking, the couples distanced themselves after a bit. Beau pulled Gracie down to sit on the sand. "Did you like your surprise, Twinkle?"

"I love it, Beau, but I loved the note even more." Beau reached over and held Gracie's hand as they laid on their backs there on the sand. It was a moment that

Gracie would always remember. She pulled out her phone and said," It's time for a selfie. Get as close as you can now."

"You don't have to tell me twice," Beau replied. He leaned in and just as Gracie clicked to take the picture, Beau kissed Gracie on the cheek. It was a picture worth a thousand words. She looked up at Beau and he said, "Gracie, I know it's too early to tell you that I love you. For now, and until a later time, I will say to you, 'I promise,' and you will know what I mean."

"Ditto for me," Gracie said as she gave Beau a gentle hug.

"I love it when you do that, Gracie. I promise," Beau said with that killer smile as he stood to pull Gracie to her feet. "Here they come, and it looks as if they are getting along very well."

"Holding hands is a good sign," Gracie added.

"Hop on my back, and I'll carry you the rest of the way back to the cottage," Beau said quietly. Gracie's small frame fit well against Beau's muscular back. Beau kissed Gracie's hand when she placed them around his neck. "Hold on!"

* * *

When they all reached the house, they planned to make an afternoon and evening out of their holiday. They would meet around two p.m. They planned to spend the entire day there until the fireworks were over. Gracie looked forward to fireworks on the beach. They could be seen for miles up and down the coastline.

"Beau, do you think we will christen your boat, Souvenir, tomorrow, so we can ride out on the water to see the fireworks better?"

Beau said, "I was going to wait since we announced it at the birthday party, but this can be our unofficial christening." Gracie, Julie, and Liam all started clapping. Beau took a bow, and they all laughed.

"See you all tomorrow," Liam said.

"Yes, until tomorrow," Beau added.

"Thank you and goodnight," Gracie said as she let go of Beau's hand.

* * *

"This is going to be a great holiday," Julie said as she walked into the cottage.

"I think it will be the best fourth of July I have had in years. No doubt about it. Hey, Julie, you can help yourself if you'd like anything to eat or drink during the night. I am going to head upstairs," Gracie said.

When Gracie hurried up the stairs and walked past the hallway mirror, she caught a glimpse of the necklace from Beau and thought of his note and promise. Never had she met anyone like Beau. She remembered the first time she met him in the market uptown. She remembered every detail of the way he looked and dressed the first time she saw him and those blue eyes and that smile. There was no way anyone could forget that.

Gracie then remembered Beau's mom telling her that Beau had never brought anyone to their home. Gracie thought that was Beau's mom telling her that this was an incredibly special event, but Gracie already knew that.

17

As Julie awoke, she could see Gracie coming up the beach from her brisk morning walk. The seagulls and shorebirds were flying overhead, and sandpipers were racing down the beach. Julie hollered out, "Ready for coffee?"

Breathless Gracie answered, "Yes!"

"Here you go, extra cream, right?" Julie asked as she handed Gracie the coffee cup, leaning out the door. "I'll be right back."

Julie walked out to model her new bikini. "Do you think this is too much?"

"It does look great on you."

"Would you wear it?" Julie asked.

"You know me. I'm always a little on the conservative side. Just do what your gut tells you!" Gracie answered.

Julie looked down at her stomach and said, "My gut is telling me to skip breakfast."

"That makes two of us. If you feel comfortable in it, then wear it! I'll just get my 1920s-style down-to-my-knees swimwear to model for you. Give me a sec." Grace hurried up the stairs to find her swimsuit. She returned with a royal blue one-piece suit. "I bought this one to match Beau's eyes. What do you think?"

"I think it's very close!"

"Me, too. This is my favorite color."

As they drank their morning coffee, Gracie's phone rang. "Hello Luv! How are things going on this wonderful Fourth of July? Any big plans?"

"Hello GiGi! I'm so glad to hear from you! My friend Julie's here with me. Beau has invited us over for a clambake and boating today," Gracie answered. "Liam was invited, too. Do you remember Liam?"

"Yes, I do! Curly blonde hair, right? Your plans sound splendid!"

"GiGi, what are your 4th of July plans in Alaska?"

"Last night, we went to the capital, Juneau, to see fireworks over the Gastineau Channel at midnight." GiGi responded. "It was quite spectacular. Fairbanks today in the land of the midnight sun for music and food in Pioneer Park. I'm not sure where we're headed after that without looking at the itinerary. Uncle John keeps us on track. Well, I won't keep you, Dear. They are waving at me to hurry up. Oh boy! Be safe! Goodbye for now!"

"Goodbye, GiGi!"

As Gracie disconnected the call, Julie asked, "I don't remember if we are driving over there today or if they are picking us up?"

"We are driving because they will be busy getting everything ready."

"It's all good. It will be so fun, and the food will be scrumptious, I'm sure! I think Liam is more excited for this feast than we are!"

"That reminds me of a cheesy biscuit recipe. What do you think?" Gracie asked. "Will it be too much?"

Julie replied, "If it is, we'll bag the biscuits up and warm them up tomorrow."

"Works for me," Gracie said. "I'll get started on those straightaway!"

* * *

After the salad and biscuits were prepared, the girls loaded up the food and headed to Water's Edge. They had already packed their towels, extra clothing, sunglasses, and SPF 15 suntan lotion. As Gracie was putting on her cover up, Julie noticed her necklace. "Is that new?"

"Yes, it's my birthday present from Beau."

"Well, girlfriend, if that is birthday, I can't wait to see Christmas!" They both cackled as they drove down the lane.

Julie asked, "Is this area part of Beau's family's estate? It's a little far from where the party was."

"I guess Beau purchased it not too long ago so he could have a place of his own."

"Wow!"

"I know."

The guys were busy preparing the area as they drove in. Gracie could see a small area where white, sugary sand was spread out by the water. She also noticed four small scooters parked by the shed.

"I hope those are sitting out so we can ride them today," Julie said. "I haven't been on one since Jr. High."

Gracie chimed in, "Me either! I think we were at your house when we rode, correct?"

Julie smiled, "You have a great memory, Gracie. Almost as good as mine!"

Gracie shook her head and noticed Beau's new sailboat, Souvenir, was sitting at the edge of the water, ready to go! Gracie could not wait to get out on that boat. She had slipped in a bottle of champagne in case Beau forgot to get one on the way.

Julie called out, "We're here!"

* * *

"We've got the drinks iced down, so please help yourself. After you get your drinks, head up to the shed, and pick out the scooter of your choice. The girls reached down and selected their beverages, then headed up to the shed.

"Hey Gracie, I'll take this bad boy!"

"You always crack me up, Julie."

The guys arrived a few minutes later. Beau said, "We thought we'd drive up the lane and look for the wild horses."

"Wild horses?" Julie asked.

"Yes, they are our best kept secret here. They are very timid, so you have to walk slowly as you approach them," Beau added.

"If we find them? Liam asked.

"No, when we find them. Let's go! I'll lead."

"Beau, are you the leader of the pack?" Julie asked.

"You are very funny, Julie."

The group drove along the path and tried to keep their voices down. They all were laughing quite a bit. It felt so good to laugh again, Julie thought.

About a mile down the lane, Beau spotted a beautiful black stallion and white mare. They were leisurely grazing in the field. One of them made a noise and then they chased each other around. The group watched them for quite a while, and Gracie tried her best to get photos. After Gracie put her phone away, a tiny white colt came from behind a fallen tree and stood near its mother.

"Do you see that?" Gracie fumbled for her phone and could not catch the Kodak moment in time before the horses heard them and galloped off down the shoreline.

"Where are they going?" Julie asked.

"We're not sure where all they go. I've only seen them about three times in my life," Liam said. "I knew this would be a special day."

"I'm not sure it can get better than that," Gracie chimed in.

Beau quickly replied with a huge smile so only Gracie could hear him, "Well, you never know." Gracie smiled back.

After about an hour, the group thought they should head back and continue getting everything going for the clambake. They wanted to have time for a quick swim before they headed out on the boat to watch the fireworks. In about an hour, everything was ready. The food was spectacular and the company even better.

"We can clean up later. Let's cannonball off this pier!" Beau announced. Everyone followed and ran to make exceptionally large splashes.

Once all the waves and splashing subsided, Liam said, "This is a wonderful place, Beau."

"Heaven on earth," Beau replied.

Liam swam over to Julie and said," I agree."

"Just what we needed to cool off. I think I'll get out and enjoy those Adirondack chairs. You coming, Beau?"

"Sure, be right there." Gracie positioned their chairs, so they had their backs to Julie and Liam since she knew their time together was short. She was amazed how well they had gotten to know each other. Julie is usually a hard sell when it comes to blind dates. Of course, she had no idea that Beau's birthday party was their blind date.

Beau reached out and held Gracie's hand while they watched the water. It was peaceful there and the weather was perfect. Neither wanted that feeling to end. Quite suddenly, a title wave of water splashed across the two of them as Liam and Julie jumped off the pier in the water right beside their chairs.

"No sleeping on the job, Beau!"

Beau stood up to jump in after Liam, then decided to sit back down. "Hey, that felt surprisingly good and reminded me that I need to be cooking. Enjoy the water."

Gracie followed Beau up to the pit area. She watched Beau skillfully bake the food. He was an expert chef in her eyes. Everything was ready in about an hour.

"I think we need a dinner bell. If you like, I will watch for one online. Would you like that, Beau?"

"I would. When we find it, let's place it over there by the shed. I can just whistle for now." Beau whistled loudly and Julie and Liam came quickly.

"Everyone, chow down!" Beau exclaimed. And

they certainly did dig in. "I'm glad to see that everyone ate at least two platefuls."

They all threw their plates in the trash and headed toward the sailboat. Gracie pulled out two small bottles of champagne - one to pour over the bow and the other to toast.

Beau said, "If you all don't mind, I am going to say a brief Boat Christening Prayer for now. "Almighty God who calmed the raging seas, we ask that you bless all who have prepared this ship for service, and especially those who named her. We ask that you protect and preserve those who will sail and surround all in your loving care. I christen thee, Souvenir!" Gracie handed Beau the tiny bottle, and he poured it over the bow, while Julie and Liam prepared the tiny toast glasses.

Gracie gathered the glasses and empty bottle and said, "Of course, we need a selfie. Everyone say cheese!"

"Everything has been checked, and the wind is blowing perfectly in the direction that we want to go All aboard! We will use the engine for a bit, then switch to just the sails when we get to where we want to be. It may take a while because we will only be travelling at a speed of about four knots."

Everyone was celebrating early with sparklers, firecrackers, bottle rockets, and all, but as the sun went down, the massive fireworks display began shooting up and down the beach.

"All aboard!" Beau called out. Everyone very excitedly filed onto the boat. The timing was perfect to be on the water. They would see an occasional dolphin and that made the trip even more special.

"Here we go!" Beau exclaimed. As they motored along the shoreline, they saw so many fireworks.

Everyone seemed to have scooters this year. The city's fireworks could be seen at a distance and were phenomenal.

"I think the fireworks get better and better," Julie said.

"It doesn't get much better than this," Liam said as he high fived the group.

As the fireworks ended, Gracie said, "I sure hate for this night to end and am glad we all have Sunday to rest before we get back to work."

"Amen to that!" Beau added.

As they sailed along, everyone shared about their new jobs and what the next week had in store for them.

"I guess we could consider this night to be our celebration for all of our new jobs and beginnings of our careers," Liam said.

"Yes, it could only had been better if my surprise for Beau had been delivered." Gracie widened her eyes and raised her eyebrows.

"Something for me? What is it?" Beau asked.

"You have to wait!" Gracie answered.

"Even if I throw you in?" Beau threatened. He hurried over and picked Gracie up and pretended that he was going to throw her in the water." What do you say now?"

"Beau!" Gracie exclaimed. All were laughing and enjoying the onboard entertainment that they were providing. "I promise you'll like it."

"You promise?" Beau asked.

* * *

It was extremely late when they arrived back home. Beau and Liam stayed to clean up and told Gracie and Julie that they would pick them up tomorrow morning for church on the beach. All agreed. Gracie kissed Beau goodnight and thanked him for such a special day. Julie hugged Liam, and he tried to pull her back a couple times as she tried to pull away to tease him.

"That Liam is something else, isn't he? Gracie asked.

"He sure is! I am so glad that I met him," Julie added. "He's pretty special."

Gracie laughed and said, "I can see that he is, Girlfriend! I'm exhausted, are you?

"Yes, exhausted in a good way, Gracie. Do you mind if we head to bed now?"

"I was thinking the same thing, Julie."

As Gracie started up the stairs, she received a text message from Beau. Goodnight and sweet dreams.

This made Gracie smile as she replied. She felt so happy and so blessed. She knew only God could know and understand this new joy in her heart. Gracie thought of one of her favorite scriptures — Psalm 37:4.

18

Beau arrived early with Liam to pick up Gracie and Julie for church on the beach. "Have either of you ever been to services on the beach?"

"I haven't," Liam said.

"Me neither. In fact, it's been a while since I have been to church. I am really looking forward to it," Julie said.

"I'll be surprised if you don't like it, guys," Gracie added.

As they were walking over to the services, they noticed that the praise service had already started. People were raising their hands and saying amen.

"I've never been to a service where the people were this excited in praise and worship,"

Julie said. "This is really different."

Gracie hoped that Julie meant different in a respectable way. She was not sure where Julie was in her walk with Christ and hoped that she would like this unique way to worship.

As the minister began to share his message about God's will for their lives and God's constant unfailing love, Julie and Liam's eyes were glued to the minister. They both barely blinked. Gracie looked at Beau, and he raised his eyebrows. Beau hoped that the message would touch Liam, because he knew that Liam had a lot of heartbreak in his family as a young child and hoped it would strike a chord of comfort for him.

When the invitation came, Julie and Liam hopped up at the same time with five others. All accepted Christ that day. Tears of joy ran down both Julie and Liam's faces as well as Gracie and Beau's. The new Christians all followed the minister to the shallow water of the sea, and they were all baptized that day in the ocean. It was such a beautiful sight. The sky was clear, and the sun was amazing.

Beau whispered to Gracie and gave her a quick squeeze, "Can you believe this today?"

"This is truly a miracle, Beau."

After the baptisms, everyone began clapping. Julie and Liam ran up to Gracie and Beau sopping wet and gave them both huge bear hugs.

"I sure didn't plan to do that today. What about you, Julie?" Liam asked.

Julie shook her head no.

"Wow, we really have a lot to talk about over lunch today, don't we?" Gracie asked.

"We sure do," Julie answered.

They decided to have lunch at one of the outdoor cafes uptown. Liam and Julie had so many questions.

"I may not be able to answer all your questions, but I do know someone who can. I'll set up some time for you next week with the pastor who baptized you today," Beau said.

"No worries, he has already scheduled some time with us next weekend. He said he will be leaving soon and wanted to be sure to talk with us," Julie said.

"I am so thankful for this day and the goodness of it all," Gracie said.

"Amen to that! Now, let's eat!" Liam chimed in.

"Now what's on the agenda this afternoon, since we can't top what happened this morning?" Beau questioned.

Julie said, "I'd like to just hang out at the beach today."

"Me, too!" Liam agreed.

"While you all are enjoying some beach time, I would like to plant my orange, lime, and lemon trees that Beau bought me."

"You're not leaving them in the planters for a while?" Beau inquired.

"No, I believe they belong in the Secret Garden," Gracie answered.

"I can help you," Beau added.

Gracie smiled and looked at Julie and Liam, who were holding hands and grinning at each other.

"Everyone like crab cakes?" Beau asked.

"Yes, yes, and yes," Gracie answered as Julie and Liam nodded their heads yes.

As the waiter came up to the table, Beau said, "Crab cakes all around, please!"

* * *

After lunch, everyone scattered for a bit. Julie and Liam went to the beach and Gracie and Beau got busy planting the trees.

"I'm so glad you decided to help me with these trees, Beau. I love them and want to make sure they get all the TLC they need."

"Gracie, they will definitely get that and then some! More memories for the Secret Garden. Let me take a picture of you with those trees," Beau said.

"Only if you are in it, Beau."

Beau said, "Ok, say cheeseburger!" as he snapped the picture.

"That was really something this morning, wasn't it, Gracie?"

"It sure is amazing to think of it."

"I knew when I met you that you were a Christian without you ever saying a word, Gracie."

"I hoped you were."

The phone rang, and it was GiGi. "Hello, Luv! I'm calling to check in."

"Hi, I'm so glad you called," Gracie said. "How are you and how is it going?"

"It has been wonderful until today. Uncle John, Aunt Ginny, and I have all become ill. The ship's captain has quarantined us to our rooms for a few days. We will only miss a couple stops. I'm sure we'll be fine, Dear. Now tell me all about you!"

Gracie gave GiGi a quick update, especially about Julie and Liam's decisions that they made this morning.

GiGi was so happy and said, "You never know how God can use you to bring others to Him just by inviting them to church on the beach! You just have to be willing to come as you are and let Him do the rest."

"That is so true, GiGi! Will you call back to give me another update in a few days?" Gracie asked.

"I sure will, Luv." GiGi began coughing. "I will have to get off here now. I love you."

"I love you and miss you, GiGi."

"What is GiGi's real name if I may ask? I always called her Mrs. Douglas before I met you," Beau inquired.

Gracie replied, "It is Gianna. Gianna Grace to be exact. You can see that I was named after her. I have always loved her name, Gianna."

"I love it and am sure I have never heard anyone call her by her first name," Beau replied.

"That's because you have good manners and since we are asking about names, what are your parents' first names?"

"When I introduced you to them, did I not use their names?"

"You did. I was just teasing you."

"For a minute, I thought I was more nervous than I realized that night! See what you do to me?"

"Well, anyway, Joel and Callista are their names. Mom is Calli for short. Now that we have that all straightened out, how about coming over here to help pack this dirt down?"

"I've got my garden boots on. What do you think?" Gracie modeled the boots as if she were on a runway.

"Beautiful! Can you grab the hose, too?"

As they were finishing planting, Liam and Julie walked around back. Liam said, "We are kind of in the mood for some homemade ice cream. I have a great family recipe if you want to end this memorable day with a great dessert."

"How soon can you get it started?" Beau asked.

"Julie and I will run to get the ingredients and the ice cream maker. I know she has to leave soon, so we will hurry."

"Sounds great!" Gracie said.

Gracie and Beau walked out to the porch and waved to them as they left. "Now come over here. There's some things I want to get straight with you, Gracie."

"And what is that Beau Bodacious?"

"Bodacious! No one has ever called me that."

Gracie chuckled and said, "Probably not to your face anyway. Seriously, your blue eyes have a language of their own."

"Well, then there are five things that I think you need to know. #1 You are more beautiful than anyone I have ever met. #2 You have the kindest heart of anyone I have ever known. #3 My life was never the same after I met you in April. #4 Your faith helps keep me strong. #5 I promise I will tell you something important in about 11 months."

Gracie leaned over and whispered in Beau's ear, "I hope I can wait until then!"

"Me too, Twinkle."

* * *

Everyone left the cottage early after ice cream since Monday was a workday for all. Gracie loved seeing the sunlight shine through the stained glass in the front window of the cottage. She thought so much about the wonderful holiday and her friends' decisions. They would all be back this weekend and she was glad. She thought of GiGi, her aunt and uncle and hoped to hear from them today. She thought it was odd that they were quarantined to their cabins.

Gracie was on her second cup of coffee and thought she'd better get to work. She knew if she would work straight through today with no breaks, other than coffee, she could be finished with work by four p.m. She missed her early morning walk and thought she would make up for it tonight. Many of the tourists would be leaving today, so she might end up having the beach to herself. She hoped Beau's surprises would be delivered this week so they could install this weekend.

Gracie knew that Beau had a busy week ahead of him. His father was anxious to hand over more business. Beau was happy that he was working from home today though. He noticed that two packages were delivered but didn't have time to see who it was for. He then thought of Gracie, the great weekend and all that happened. It was hard to focus on work, but he knew he must.

GiGi called around noon to let Gracie know that they were going to let them stay aboard for the remainder of their trip. Many of the passengers who ate the shrimp at one of the pre-holiday parties ended up with food poisoning. They were all feeling much better now and ready to explore the unknown and then some.

Gracie was worried about them, but knew they were safe. She pulled out her bunny slippers and started happily to work.

19

The next few weeks passed very quickly and GiGi, Aunt Ginny, and Uncle John returned home early. Gracie had to drive to Aunt Ginny's house to pick her up.

"We have lots to talk about on the way home, Gracie."

GiGi wanted Gracie to know that she had made some major decisions while she was away. Primarily, GiGi's plan was to move in with her sister to help take care of her. Aunt Ginny had a few health issues and just needed someone to help her at home. She would also be closer to Uncle John since he lived in the same town. They had such an exciting time together, they wanted it all to continue, especially when they considered their ages.

Secondly, GiGi was ready to sign over the cottage to Gracie. It was becoming too much work for her, and she was ready to be inland for a while.

Thirdly, GiGi told Gracie that Aunt Ginny's home had lots of room for her to stay there when she had to come in to work at the office as needed.

Gracie asked, "Do I have any say in this?"

GiGi replied, "I'm afraid not, Dear. The hand is already shuffled, and you have already won."

"What do you mean? You won't be here," Gracie

said.

"I will always be close by, Luv, but we actually have four more trips planned before the end of the year. You can come along if you like."

Gracie handed GiGi the memory book that she made her with all the pictures that she had sent Gracie while she was gone. "If you like this, we can make one for Aunt Ginny and Uncle John." Gracie was quiet the rest of the way home. She was upset by this change. It was too much to take in right now.

* * *

Beau received both of his surprise packages on the same day and was incredibly excited and called Gracie.

"I have two packages here, one small and one large. Do you know anything about them?"

"I sure do!"

"Do you mind coming over so I can open them?"

"Sure, I'll be right over."

Gracie grabbed her keys and headed over to the Jackson Estate.

When she arrived, the gates were open. Beau was outside with a boxcutter knife ready to go.

"Can you hold the box when I am cutting the big box first?"

"Yes, can you guess what it is?"

Beau started cutting very slowly. When he finally was able to pull the sides off, he could not believe it. "I have always wanted one of these! Where in the world did you find it?"

"I wanted to find something special for you to

put out on Water's Edge Lane. I hope it works. It's pretty old."

"I think I can have one of my friends help me get it mounted out there this weekend. Thank you so much. I really love it. Now for package number two."

"You may not be as excited about this one."

"If you picked it out, it will be perfect and it is! I needed this for my on-site office. I just received my business cards today."

"I would like one, please," Gracie said.

Beau teased, "I'll even write my personal cell number on the back for you."

"Oh you! I need to get back home and back to work. See you later? Beau, I've got some news to share, but it can wait."

"Pick you up at six?" Beau asked.

"Yes, see you then."

"Bye, Gracie."

Beau was ecstatic about his gifts from Gracie. He thought, *"She was so considerate and gives everything from the heart."* Beau decided he would have to get something for Gracie for their six months together anniversary that was coming up. He wanted something exceptionally special.

* * *

Beau promptly arrived at the cottage at six and Gracie was waiting outside for him. GiGi was on the phone scheduling her movers for next month. GiGi waved at Beau and continued talking.

"Must be important, huh?"

Gracie replied, I'll tell you all about it when we

get there."

"Where?" Beau asked.

"Wherever you want to go," Gracie replied.

Beau drove around for a while and decided to park uptown around the square.

"What would you like to drink, Gracie?"

"Whatever you're having."

"All righty then. I'll be right back."

When Beau returned, Gracie filled him in on all that GiGi had told her and how disappointed she was. He tried to console her, but she couldn't see past GiGi's move at this moment.

"Gracie, you have to think about it like this: picture you and GiGi standing on a line with marks all the way down the line. Each mark equals ten years. Place yourself on the mark where your age is. Now look to the left and see how much time you have lived. Now look to the right and see how much time you might have left to live. Now look at GiGi's time left. There's a significant difference, isn't there? GiGi has a lot to add in the short distance left on that line. Does that make sense?"

"Yes, I never really thought about it that way. Thanks for making me see how selfish I am."

"You know that wasn't the point, Twinkle."

"I know."

"Feel better about it?"

"Yes."

"We'll just have to join them on some of their trips," Beau said." Where all are they going?"

"They are going on four more this year, but I

haven't heard where all they're going to! Can you believe it? That's more trips than I have been on in the last decade!" Gracie shook her head and began to laugh.

"What would I do without you, Beau?"

"I guess we'll never know! Ready to head back now?" Gracie nodded.

When they pulled into the drive, GiGi was outside with a freshly brewed pitcher of sweet, iced tea and homemade bread and strawberry jelly. "I was needing a pick-me-up this afternoon. You, too?"

"No thank you, Mrs. Douglas."

"GiGi, now tell us where you are going on all of these upcoming trips!"

"In August, we are heading to Maine to see the lighthouses. In September, we are going to Texas to hear my two favorite Texan pastors preach. In October, back to the East Coast for autumn color. In November we'll be flying to Seattle and driving down to the coast of California. December is home for the holidays. It kind of makes me tired thinking of all of that. I also have to be moved before all of the travelling starts!"

"Did you get your movers scheduled?" Beau asked.

"Yes, they are a local company, and I am so glad," GiGi said.

"My friends and I can help if you need an extra hand."

"Thank you, Beau! Now, Gracie and Beau, how are your new jobs going?"

Gracie and Beau took turns talking about their new jobs and how they both loved telecommuting. GiGi noticed Gracie's necklace. "What's that there around your neck, Luv?"

"It was a surprise from Beau. Isn't it beautiful?"

"Well, I'd say so! Come closer so I can see it better." Gracie leaned in so GiGi could examine.

"You have very good taste, young man!"

"Especially in women, don't you think, GiGi?"

"I know so!" GiGi answered with a huge smile and belly laugh.

"GiGi, Beau checked the cottage for me a couple times when we came in late and noticed Gramma Sophie's Book of Poetry. I let him know that you wouldn't mind if he read it, but the book cannot leave the property."

"Hmmm, it's a very important book to me, but because it's Beau asking, I might allow it once." Gracie and Beau were shocked.

"Why, thank you, Mrs. Douglas. I will take particularly loving care of it and return it in a day if that is okay?"

"Beau, you can keep it two days if you like. Sometime when you are here a little longer, I will tell you both the story about Gramma Sophie's quilts."

"We would love that, GiGi."

20

GiGi's move to her new home went very smoothly as well as her monthly excursions with her brother and sister. Life was good for all of them. Christmas was around the corner, and Beau had a plan. He wasn't sure Gracie would go along with it, but he would see. He knew he had made a promise to her a year from the date of their birthdays. His heart hoped for a change in the promise. Beau wanted to take Gracie to those palm trees on December 25th and propose. Together, they would choose an engagement ring. The promise would be to start planning their wedding on their next birthdays. He prayed Gracie would agree. At some point, he wanted to ask GiGi for her hand in marriage before the 25th. Beau felt badly for Gracie, thinking of her getting married without her parents. She has her GiGi, Aunt Ginny, and Uncle John. Soon, she will have Beau's parents, too. They adored Gracie.

* * *

Gracie was busy planning a small New Year's Party at the beach in between doing research work for her company. She loved her work. Beau stopped and she shared some of the details with him. He was glad some of their local friends would be able to come, as well as Julie and Liam who were still doing well with their long-distance relationship.

"Will you be able to come to my house Christmas evening?" Beau asked.

"Yes, if you can come with me to GiGi's Christmas Eve for lunch?"

"I wouldn't miss it," Beau said.

"You'll have to tell me more about your family's Christmas customs and whether I need to prepare food, gifts, or anything else?"

"Just bring yourself. Mom will have everything prepared. We almost have as many lights as Silver Dollar City at Christmas time!"

"I can't wait to see it, Beau. Now let's talk more about this New Year's Eve party that we are hosting."

* * *

Beau made a special trip to see GiGi without Gracie knowing. They met at one of GiGi's favorite restaurants so she could order coconut cream pie, which was Beau's favorite too. "I have something important to talk to you about, Mrs. Douglas."

"What is it, Dear? Are your parents well?" GiGi asked.

"They are fine. I'm a little nervous so please excuse me for bumbling my words if I do. Here goes. Gracie and I met last spring, and she's like no one else that I have met in my life. I can't imagine life without her, and I love her."

A small tear welled up in GiGi's eye. "I know you do, Dear. I could tell that the first time I saw you together. Sometimes you just know."

"I would like to ask you for her hand in marriage."

"My dear boy, even though it's only been six months, I completely give you both my blessing. Does she know yet?"

"No, she doesn't yet. We had talked about getting engaged a year from our birthdays, but I would like to see our engagement in December and wedding in June. I really don't know if she will agree, since we haven't known each other that long."

"The heart knows what we don't know sometimes. Now please tell me again when you are going to pop the question?"

"Christmas night at my parent's home. There are three palm trees where I made the original promise to her, and I want to take her there again for this."

"I will be praying for God to lead you both at this especially crucial time in your lives. Now, please call me GiGi." GiGi stood up and gave Beau a big hug. "There is one thing that I want to tell you and you must keep it a secret. Do you agree?"

"Yes, of course."

"Gracie's mother left her one more gift. She cannot receive it until she has her first child though. Do you promise that you will keep this secret until that day comes? It's a message that her mother left her in a bottle that she found on the beach."

"I will, GiGi."

As Beau drove back home, he wondered what the message could be.

* * *

Beau was on pins and needles all Christmas Day. He hadn't gotten much sleep the night before from staying up late and playing games at GiGi's on Christmas Eve. The time was here. Gracie would be here in ten minutes. He walked out to check the area to ensure the path was clear out to the three palm trees and it was. His mom had added a little bench out there, so they could sit and talk if they wanted to.

Gracie pulled up right on time. The Christmas lights were magnificent, and she could see the glow from a mile away. Beau went out to greet her as she walked in. "I brought your parents a bottle of red wine for dinner. Do your parents drink wine?"

"Yes, on special occasions. It will be a pleasant surprise. I hope you are hungry! Look at this spread!"

When Gracie walked in, everything was beautifully decorated, and it really put her in the Christmas spirit. "I can see where you get your good taste, Beau." There were a few other family members there that Gracie remembered from the birthday party.

"After we eat, I want to show you something outside, Gracie."

"All right!"

Gracie didn't think she had ever seen so much food. After Beau's father said the blessing, Beau started to dig in. "I have been waiting for this and you all day."

Gracie followed him through the line and filled her plate, mostly with appetizers and desserts. "This pecan pie is amazing!" Gracie exclaimed. "Is it an old family recipe?"

Beau answered, "Yes, it is. Let me see if I can get a copy for you. Are you done now?"

Gracie could see that Beau was a little nervous

and edgy. "What's going on? Are you doing okay?"

"Here's your jacket." Beau held out his hand and said, "Come with me."

Gracie got up and took Beau's hand. He was not himself tonight and she was a little worried about him. When they got outside by the palm trees, Beau said, "You can sit down if you like."

Gracie sat down and Beau got down on one knee and took both of Gracie's hands in his and kissed them. "Gracie, I really wanted to wait to fulfill our promise next summer. Summer seems so far away to me." Gracie's eyes widened. "Will you marry me next summer and get engaged tonight?"

Gracie was speechless. Her heart was saying yes, and her mind was saying no.

Beau looked Gracie in the eyes and said, "I know we haven't known each other as long as some people before they get engaged, but I knew very soon that I wanted to marry you. I have had perfect peace about this decision and hope you feel the same." Beau looked down because Gracie paused. She took his face in her hands and said, "Yes, yes, a thousand times, yes."

Beau got up off his knees and picked Gracie up and sat her on his lap. They embraced for several minutes, then Beau said, "I cannot wait until you are my wife. I love you, Twinkle."

"I love you so much, Beau."

They both smiled from ear to ear. Beau said, "Gracie, I want to take you to pick out your ring together."

"That would be perfect, Beau. Will we tell our

families tonight?"

"Yes, I'm so glad you brought the wine. We have more celebrating to do."

Gracie and Beau walked back in the house holding hands. Gracie could feel everyone's eyes on them. "I have an announcement to make! I have proposed to the love of my life tonight and she accepted!"

The whole family swarmed the couple. They shared their engagement stories, along with congratulations and well wishes. Gracie couldn't wait to get home to call GiGi to tell her.

Gracie whispered, "Beau, do you think we could go somewhere so I can call GiGi to tell her?"

"Yes, let's go to the study. It's quiet in there."

Gracie called to tell GiGi all the details of the way the night transpired. GiGi was ecstatic! Beau came clean that he had already spoken to GiGi about proposing but wasn't sure if Gracie would say yes. They all had a good laugh about that.

"Six months isn't long to plan a wedding, Luv. We need to get together soon."

Gracie and Beau agreed, but they would be happy to elope.

"We will be ring shopping next weekend, GiGi, but we can start planning the next weekend if you like?"

"Sounds great. I will tell Uncle John and Aunt Ginny to not schedule any trips for May and June. We are going to be terribly and wonderfully busy."

As Gracie shared the update, GiGi, said. I love you both." Her voice cracked as she said goodbye.

* * *

Beau's parents asked Gracie to stay the night at their house. They have a guest suite that would be perfect for her. Beau offered Gracie one of his t-shirts to sleep in.

Callista suggested that Beau ride with Gracie to get an overnight bag. She added, "We'd really love it if you stayed with us tonight."

Gracie hadn't thought about being alone on Christmas night, and she gladly accepted.

Gracie drove the convertible and as they were pulling out of the drive, Beau stood up and yelled," This girl is going to marry me, and I can't wait! I love her!" Gracie was so happy.

When they arrived at the cottage, Beau wanted to go in to check everything out. He always worried about her being there by herself since GiGi moved. "All clear!"

Gracie hopped up the stairs to get her things and came down with a small bag.

"You sure do pack light! That's another thing I love about you and yes, I did say love."

"We'd better not be too long, or they will worry. Wouldn't you love to be a little mouse to hear all that they are saying?" Gracie asked.

"I know it's all good, soon-to-be-Mrs. Jackson. Let's go!"

* * *

Beau's family slept in after the late night, and Gracie was glad. As she laid there, she noticed a beautiful hand-stitched quilt under the comforter on the bed. It looked remarkably similar to some of Gramma

Sophie's hand-stitched quilts. Gracie thought the pattern might be double wedding ring.

Beau came to her room early and said, "Are you decent? Do you need a robe or anything?"

"A robe would be nice if you are coming in," Gracie replied.

"I just happen to have one! It's mine so it may be a little small for you."

"You are so funny! Come on in then!"

Beau handed her a robe and turned around while she put it on. "One of these days, I won't have to turn around, Twinkle."

"Beau!"

* * *

Gracie had to pinch herself as she was driving home. She never dreamed her life could be anything like it was in this moment and the moments to come. God had everything laid out in a perfect plan for her and Beau. They both just had to have faith to step out and grab it and each other.

Gracie had so many questions about their future. Would they get matching wedding rings? Would they live in the cottage? Would they continue working in their current jobs? How many people would they invite to the wedding? Where will the wedding be? She made herself stop thinking about it all and told herself, "It's all in God's plan."

She had quite a bit of work to do when she arrived home after being off work for the holidays. She looked forward to keeping her mind occupied. She knew once GiGi had time to think about things, it would get fantastically interesting fast!

There was one thing that she wanted for sure and that was Beau in a tux. She also wanted her dress to be quite simple and elegant. She thought about bird of paradise or magnolias in her bouquet. The rest of the planning didn't matter that much as far as the size of the wedding and reception, the decorations, and the food. She did want a groom's cake with a sailboat named Souvenir on it.

Beau called to set a date for engagement ring shopping which was Saturday all day until they found what they wanted.

21

Gracie could see Beau coming up the drive. He seemed to hop up five stairs at a time. She had never seen him move like that before. "I've got a couple places in mind to look. My dad mentioned his jeweler where he buys all my mom's jewelry. Dad said the man is fair and won't try to talk you into anything that isn't what you want. Do you want to go there?"

"Beau, I want you to know that I would be happy with just a solid wide wedding band."

"I know you would, Gracie. To me, though, I want you to always see me every time you take a glimpse of your hand. I'll always be here with you, Twinkle. "Beau, if that is what you want. Now, let's start there if your dad trusts this gentleman so much."

"I will let Dad know. That will please him. We've got to keep up the Jackson family traditions, you know!"

Once they arrived, the owner of the store met them at the door and introduced himself and started showing them around. "This is what we have in stock. If there is anything you would like uniquely created, please let me know. Beau's father says I have a knack for creating unique jewelry. Take your time. I will be in the back."

"I don't need to look any further, Beau. Do you see what I see?"

"I think so. I'll point to it to see if we are on the same page." Beau pointed to the same ring that Gracie had zeroed in on.

"That's amazing that we both saw and liked the same ring out of over one hundred rings!"

"Did you find one?" the jeweler asked.

Beau answered, pointing, "Yes, we'd like the emerald cut one, but please see if we can add two more carats to make it 3.01. May we try it on?"

Beau noticed that Gracie's hand was shaking and held it while the jeweler had his associate bring out the rings.

"Very good choice and fit! That is exceedingly rare. You have small fingers."

"I love it, Beau. Can we afford it?"

"We are getting it, if that's the one, whatever it costs. Please prepare it for us. When can we pick it up?"

"Did you want the set and the matching groom's ring?"

"Is that what we want, Gracie?"

"Yes." Beau leaned down and sealed the deal with a soft kiss right on Gracie's lips in front of the jeweler and his associate. Beau had never done anything like that in his life.

* * *

The wedding plans were coming along nicely. Between GiGi and Callista, things seemed to be going very well. Gracie's only request was to keep it small. By small, she meant one hundred or less guests. Gracie and Beau both wanted to say their vows by the three palm trees and did not care in the least about a big wedding venue. Gracie hoped Beau would stick to his guns and not let them talk him into something else.

Their next item to check off the list was the wedding gown, maid of honor dress and tuxes for the three guys. Gracie had already asked Julie to be her maid of honor and Beau had asked Liam to be his best man. Uncle John would walk her down the aisle. GiGi booked the appointment for the dresses and fittings the next weekend. Time was running out for any item that had to be altered. GiGi had told Gracie that she, Aunt Ginny, and Uncle John were paying for the wedding as their wedding gift to them. GiGi also said that she was waiting to sign the cottage over to Gracie after her name changed to save her more legal work. Gracie was so relieved and couldn't wait to tell Beau.

* * *

On the dress fitting day, Team Gracie all showed up: GiGi, Aunt Ginny, Callista, and Julie. Gracie had tried on about five dresses. She saved her favorite for last. When she walked out to model the dress, there wasn't a dry eye.

"Does it look that bad?" Gracie teased.

"They all began clapping and said in unison, "That's the one!"

As Gracie was walking back to the dressing room, Callista asked Gracie to wait on her. As they walked toward the dressing room, Callista said, "May I have a moment with you Gracie?"

"Yes, of course, Callista," Gracie answered.

"From the depths of our hearts, Joel and I want to welcome you into our family and want you to know that we will always think of you as our daughter now." I know your early losses in life have been great, but your future just added a whole other family, and we welcome you with open arms."

Gracie and Callista both teared up, and Gracie answered, "Thank you, Callista. My heart is full." Callista hugged Gracie.

"I must get back to the girls and find a dress myself! I loved the designs and colors that you selected for us."

"Gracie, we have prayed for someone like you for a long time for Beau."

Gracie reached out one hand to squeeze Callista's hand and wiped her eyes with the other.

* * *

Thankfully, by April, everything was amazingly completed. Gracie couldn't believe the great teamwork by both families and friends. Gracie and Beau already had their time off requests approved for their honeymoon. Beau had secured their honeymoon reservations and would not tell her where they were going as a surprise. He knew Gracie loved surprises.

Gracie and Beau were so anxious to get their new life started. Beau and his father helped make a few maintenance upgrades on the cottage since Gracie and Beau would be living there after the wedding. The important thing about Water's Edge Lane was that it butted up next to GiGi's property line. Months ago, GiGi had given Beau the heads up that the property was for sale, and he bought it that day.

* * *

May was an incredibly busy month for the couple. There were wedding showers and last-minute wedding items to complete. Gracie didn't stress about any of it though. She told Beau she did not want to be a bridezilla. He said he wanted this day to be the happiest day of her life thus far, and he promised he wouldn't be a groomzilla.

All wedding plans were finally completed, and the destination of the wedding would be by the three palm trees in Beau's back yard where he proposed. Beau wanted to be able to point at those trees some day in the future and tell their children, "Right over there by those three palm trees is where I asked your mother to marry me and when she said yes, that is where we actually were married." Another thing that she loved about Beau.

There was plenty of room for one hundred guests, wedding arbor, and large gazebo and canopy tent. The setting by the water was perfect for a wedding and was so serene. Beau's mother had such a gift for planning and decorating. She wanted to line the drive with luminaries to guide everyone up the drive and into the backyard area.

Gracie and Beau had been meeting regularly for several days specifically to finalize their wedding vows. They felt this was the most important part of their wedding day. They wanted their vows to be meaningful and true and finally agreed on the following:

"You are my lover and my best friend.
You are my soul's destination.
I will love you, hold you, and honor you.

*I will respect you, encourage you, and cherish you
In sickness and in health.
Through sorrows and successes
All the days of my life."*

22

Gracie awoke early to the aroma of GiGi's coffee brewing. It was barely sunrise. She was tired from the wedding rehearsal dinner the night before and knew that coffee would give her the spark that she needed for the day. The happiest day of her life. She walked over to the top of the staircase and sat down. Gracie always loved seeing the sunlight through the stained-glass window and wanted to savor every minute that she had with GiGi. After today, everything would be different. She listened as GiGi went about in the kitchen singing to herself. Gracie could smell the cinnamon rolls baking in the oven.

Gracie slid down the banister for good luck and walked over to get some coffee.

"My, you haven't done that in a while!"

"Actually, I do it on special days. Thank goodness it's very sturdy."

"Awww, your mama used to do that when she was eight years old!"

GiGi laughed with that wonderful belly laugh, and Gracie almost spit out her coffee. She loved the fact that GiGi kept Mama's memory alive with stories about her as things reminded her of her only child.

Gracie looked up and noticed that GiGi had placed a heart around the 25th. "Today's the big day,

Luv. I have something for you." GiGi opened a drawer and pulled out the most beautiful lace handkerchief with blue print. "Do you remember that wedding tradition, something old, something new, something borrowed, and something blue – Sixpence in your shoe? Well, your dress is the new and the lace handkerchief is the old, borrowed, and blue.

Gracie added, "Our best man has a royal blue vest and cummerbund, and my maid of honor will be in the same shade of blue. I believe you and Beau's mother are wearing blue dresses as well?"

"Yes, that is right, Dear. Here is the sixpence for Beau's shoe. They don't make the sixpence coins any longer so be sure to keep it in a safe place to be passed on to your children, along with the lace handkerchief. Gramma Sophie's mother started these family traditions when Gramma Sophie got married in 1951. Both items and traditions have been passed down through four generations now with you. I don't know if you realized it, but all of us were June brides. Can you believe it?"

Gracie was already a little emotional today, but that sure did it. Gracie hugged her grandmother and told her that she didn't know what she would do if she wasn't here with her today. GiGi and Gracie both wiped a few tears from their eyes as they sat back down. She thought of her parents and wished so that they were here.

"It will be a wonderful day, Luv. Just relax and enjoy it. If things don't go exactly right, it may lighten the mood and make others laugh. When your mother and father were married, Papa was at the alter to give your mother away. As he was coming back to sit with me, Papa tripped over the train of your mama's wedding dress. Luckily, he caught himself, so he didn't fall. There wasn't a dry eye in the place. You know, Papa was always the life of the party."

"I had never heard that story! Thank you, GiGi. It means so much to me, especially today."

"Today will be perfect however it goes - just like you, Luv."

* * *

Gracie could see the guests arriving in the outside terrarium by the event. She really wasn't nervous because GiGi, Julie, and Beau's mother were there helping Gracie with her dress, makeup, and hair.

It was time for the ceremony to begin, so GiGi and Callista headed toward the house to be escorted to sit in the front. The music began and Gracie felt the butterflies starting. "Are you all right, Gracie? Julie asked. "How about some water?"

"That would be wonderful."

"Now stand up and let's take a selfie in the mirror before all the excitement begins." Gracie stood up and saw herself for the first time since the dress fitting. "You clean up rather good, girlfriend. The guys are coming in now. Oh my, look at Liam!"

Gracie sighed and said, "Look at Beau!" She had never seen him look so happy and handsome. His blue eyes were shining brighter than his perfect smile. Just then, there was a knock at the door. It was Uncle John. He was standing in for Gracie's dad.

"Here we go, Gracie!" Julie picked up Gracie's

bouquet, handed it to her, and gave her a wink. She then picked up her own flowers and headed to the door. Uncle John came in and stopped in the doorway.

"Gracie, I have never seen a more beautiful bride than you. Are you ready?" Gracie nodded. The wedding processional started to begin, and everyone stood up. The photographer snapped a quick photo of Beau when he saw Gracie for the first time in her wedding gown. "Did you see Beau's face when he saw you?" Gracie nodded.

The wedding ceremony and vows were so meaningful. Gracie could hear a few sniffles in the audience behind her. She was doing well until that moment. She could feel a tear falling down her cheek. She looked over at Beau, and he had tears down both cheeks. He squeezed her hand and that made her feel much better.

"And now, I would like to introduce Mr. and Mrs. Beau Jackson. The couple would like to meet and greet you at your seats as you are leaving to thank you for coming. The reception will immediately follow. We will all gather at the entrance of the reception to 'bubble' the new couple into the reception. Thank you and God bless."

Gracie and Beau greeted all the guests and most of them stayed for the reception. The maid of honor and best man planned a fun reception. Their toasts for the wedding couple were so heart felt by all, acknowledging the memory table that GiGi and Callista created for those who were in Heaven. Gracie felt that this was truly a divine appointment planned and maneuvered by God himself.

Uncle John was happy to dance with Gracie for the father-daughter dance. Beau's mother was so beautiful in her blue dress and was light on her feet. She could see Beau's father looking at her like he was in love with her all over again. Uncle John kept the conversation light and told Gracie they would talk about work again when they got back from their honeymoon. Gracie knew her work contract would end soon and wondered what he had in mind.

At the end of the father-daughter dance, Beau came over and tapped Uncle John on the shoulder and asked Gracie if he could have this forever dance. She curtsied and he bowed. Everyone got a kick out of seeing that. Beau pulled Gracie close and said, "I love you, Twinkle, and I always will." Gracie looked up at Beau and gave him a G-rated quick kiss and told him there was more where that came from. Beau squeezed her tighter and whispered back, "I'm glad we waited."

The orchestra leader invited all to join the couple on the dance floor. Everyone danced the night away, even GiGi, Uncle John, Aunt Ginny, and especially Beau's parents, who were magnificent dancers. When they glided close to Gracie and Beau, Gracie said, "You two are delightful dancers!"

Beau's father laughed and replied, "Those ballroom dancing lessons that Callista signed us up for really paid off!"

"Dad, you are hilarious. Thanks, Mom!" Beau replied.

Callista smiled and gave Joel a big kiss on the

cheek. Joel added, "That's why I do what I do." They all chuckled and continued dancing.

GiGi walked over to remind the couple to throw the bouquet and garter. "Thank you GiGi. We almost forgot!" Everyone lined up to catch each item. Julie caught the bouquet, and Liam caught the garter. Seemed a little suspicious, but everyone clapped and patted them on the back.

The crowd started to dwindle down to only a handful of guests, mostly family and friends. Beau's best man, Liam, leaned over to Beau and said, "Your limo has arrived, and your bags are being loaded as we speak."

"You are the man! Thank you for everything that you have done for us. I guess you are next since you caught Gracie's garter and Julie caught her bouquet!"

"Oh, is that what that means?" Liam taunted.

"Really, thanks, man," Beau said as he hugged and high-fived his friend.

Gracie was thanking Julie at the same time when Beau started to usher her toward the limo. "Beau, we need to properly thank our family again before we go." The couple hugged and thanked all of those who made the wedding possible and those who were still there. Uncle John asked her to take a group selfie of all of them for their memory books since they were all dressed up and looked so good.

Gracie snorted and made everyone else laugh, then said, "You've got it! Send it to me, please, Uncle John!"

Uncle John looked at GiGi and Aunt Ginny and

said, "Well, there goes our girl."

"Let's go, Gracie! Your chariot awaits!" Beau was becoming a little impatient because he was so excited to get started on their honeymoon.

The wedding photographer took a quick photo once the couple was in the car. "I don't think I have ever taken a more beautiful picture in my career," the photographer said. I would like to display it in my business window uptown if you don't mind?" He showed them the picture.

"Wow, is that us? Gracie asked and they both giggled.

"It sure is. Congratulations, you two."

"Thank you," Beau said politely and closed the door. "Off we go to the Island of Crete! Now come here, you!"

As they started to drive away, Julie stopped the Chauffer and added a sign on the back of the car that read, "And they lived happily ever after." Gracie and Beau looked at each other, then back at the crowd, as guests waved wildly while the limo drove passed the luminaries and through the iron gate.

23

Gracie hated thinking of packing to return home after such a memorable honeymoon. Every time she would start to pack, Beau would pull the clothes back out of the suitcase and chase Gracie around the room. Beau would always say, "Who needs clothes on your honeymoon? Just get your bikini on! They would laugh and pick them up again.

Soon it would be time to get back to reality, but not quite yet. Gracie wanted to surprise Beau with a very memorable trip to another location on the island for an overnight stay. Staying in Santorini would be extremely hard to top, but she wanted to try. She had remembered Beau mentioning pink sand on one of their walks along the beach when they first met. She imagined and planned a 2-day trip to include traveling to Zakynthos, where the Navagio Shipwreck Beach is. She scheduled the glass bottom boat cruise, turtle spotting, and a walk to the private coves that would serve them nicely as they made memories worth repeating.

The following day they took a ferry trip to 2014's one of twenty-five Best Beaches, Elafonissi Beach. It would definitely fit the bill. The crushed shells of sea creatures called foraminifera lived on the coral reef to create the pink powdery sand. At low tide, they walked the beach to a secluded cove for their last sunset there.

Gracie thought that this would be the perfect place to exchange their wedding gifts to each other since they had decided to wait until the last night of their honeymoon to do so.

The gifts were not a surprise because they had ordered each other matching Bibles. Beau's Bible was black leather and Gracie's was white leather. Both were engraved on the front cover with Song of Songs 8:6-7 and on the back cover with Ecclesiastes 4:9-12. They promised to pray and read the Bible daily together, whatever was going on in their lives. They knew this would be the solid foundation of their marriage.

When they finally arrived at Elafonissi Beach, Beau was overwhelmed with the huge surprise and loved the pink sand. "What will you think of next, Gracie? I don't want this to ever end." He pulled Gracie close as the silhouette of their bodies became one while they took in all of God's beauty in this magnificent place.

"I hope we always feel like this, Beau, Gracie whispered.

"We will, Twinkle."

* * *

Gracie had no idea, but Beau had a few more surprises in store for her when they returned home at Water's Edge Lane. He had planned and scheduled the local florist to build a pergola amidst four arbor arches and to plant wisteria and other native plants around them. They planted assorted colors because he knew that Gracie loved wisteria and it would provide some seclusion and shade. Beau also knew that the wisteria would attract various area butterflies and moths, so that was a double positive. He thought they could add an outside bar at a later time for the many parties and get togethers in the future with family and friends.

24

The newlyweds arrived home to many wedding gifts and boxes of Beau's clothes. They had planned to get the remainder of his personal items at a later time from his parents' home. The cottage was quaint, not allowing much space for additional personal items, but they didn't care. Right now, they had each other and didn't need much more. Beau swept Gracie up in the traditional way that a bride is carried over the threshold. The kiss lasted a little longer than expected, and Beau had a little trouble balancing.

"Whoa, are you a little woozy? A little weak in the knees, Beau?"

"Well, maybe!"

It reminds me of the first time you surprised me in GiGi's backyard. I didn't know what had hit me at that moment."

"Me either, Gracie."

"I sure didn't expect you to carry me over the threshold twice – our honeymoon night and our first time in our home as newlyweds!"

With that, they moved on into the cottage.

"It's so good to be home with you, Gracie!"

"It's so good to be home, Beau! Now, come here and I'll give you a backrub."

"That would be great, maybe after supper? I'll

grill out for us while there's still daylight. What are you hungry for? Shish-ka-bobs with steak or shrimp?"

"Whatever you are having. I'll fix a salad and get some fresh corn on the cob out of the garden."

"Perfect!" Beau agreed.

After dinner was ready, Beau reached out to hold Gracie's hands while he said the blessing. He thanked God for how He had blessed them by bringing them together, having been given such a beautiful home, and for safety while they were overseas.

"Amen!" they both said at the same time.

While they were eating, Beau brought up getting back to work soon.

"I guess we should maybe talk about our home office set ups. Do you prefer that I work from the corporate office, so I won't crowd you?" Beau inquired.

"I think with three bedrooms, we have enough room for another home office if you like?"

"That would be fine if it's doable."

"We definitely can make it work," Gracie said as she squeezed Beau's hand. I am kind of surprised that the phone hasn't started ringing yet."

"I'm surprised no one has stopped by yet."

"Let's hope our company waits until tomorrow. I want you all to myself, Mrs. Jackson."

* * *

Beau had been curled around Gracie and had pulled her up next to him while they slept in perfect slumber. Gracie woke early and laid in bed, savoring the moment. Beau was resting so peacefully, and she loved to hear the rhythm of his breathing. He was so handsome, and she loved looking at him and admiring his perfect physique.

The sun was just beginning to rise up over the water and the waves were steady. Beau had left the French doors open to their bedroom so they could hear the waves crashing to shore and smell the salty breezes while enveloped in the sheets. Gracie again felt she almost had to pinch herself to be sure that all of this was real.

The phone rang around 8 a.m. and woke Beau up. It was GiGi checking to ensure that Gracie and Beau made it home safely. GiGi's call was followed up by Beau's parents calling, then Julie and Liam. All were checking to make sure all was well. Beau's mother, Callista offered to invite everyone over to their home the following weekend, so Gracie and Beau could share with them almost all about the honeymoon, leaving out the best parts, of course. Beau agreed that they would be able to come.

When he got off the phone, he told Gracie, "I have one more surprise for you after seeing everyone at my parents' home this weekend."

"Another surprise? Beau, you are spoiling me?"

Beau's blue eyes sparkled, and he answered, "That's my job now."

"I'm glad," Gracie responded with a huge smile. Now how about that back rub?"

* * *

The weekend get together was so much fun. GiGi had brought Uncle John and Aunt Ginny along to the cookout at the Jackson's home. They had been remarkably busy planning their next trip to Maine for the autumn lighthouse tour. They would start in Portland, Maine, and travel south to New Hampshire, seeing at least thirty lighthouses in seven days. Gracie hoped to see those lighthouses someday.

Julie and Liam were late arriving due to some work issues that had to be resolved first. They wanted to hear all about the honeymoon, so Beau said he would update them when they went over to Water's Edge.

Beau's parents were so accommodating to everyone and made wonderful appetizers and finger foods for the get together. Gracie said, "I think this beef fondue is one of my favorites that you make, Callista."

"Do you mean Fondue Bourguignonne?" Beau asked.

"Yes, I guess that is the correct name for it, ha. Will you share your recipe with me?"

"I would love to, Gracie," Callista answered.

"Wait until you try her beef wellington, Joel replied. It's a New Year's Eve favorite."

"I am anxious to try it," Gracie quickly replied.

"Will you tell us about your family dish, Sophie's Special?" Callista asked.

GiGi quickly answered, "It was my mother's recipe. Gramma Sophie would fix it when Gracie and her mother, Joy, would come to visit. It was Gracie's favorite, wasn't it, Luv?"

"Yes, I still love it," Gracie said with a smile.

"I love it too!" Beau exclaimed.

"We love it, too!" Julie added. Gracie fixed it for all of us recently, and we all knew we definitely wanted it again."

"Well, I hope you ladies will share your recipe with me," Callista said.

"We sure will, but for now, let's get back to this beef fondue," Beau said as he picked up a fondue skewer.

While they were all eating, Beau shared about the pink sand and how he loved the glass bottom boat ride that they took. Gracie pulled seven small sea turtles out of a bag and shared about how they were able to see the sea turtles there. Gracie laughed and named them the seven dwarfs. As Gracie handed them out, Beau named them all to match their owners appropriately. They all cackled.

Uncle John spoke up and said, "I guess that makes Gracie and you, Snow White and the Handsome Prince?"

Beau laughed and twirled Gracie around and said, "Ha, Ha! Maybe so!"

* * *

After cleaning up dinner and telling everyone goodnight, Beau excused himself, Gracie, Julie, and Liam to head over to Water's Edge.

"Before you go, we have one more gift that has been in the family for four generations now, counting you and Beau. Beau said that you love quilts."

Gracie's eyes widened. "Is this the quilt that was on the bed I slept in?"

"Yes, it is."

"Oh my, I love it. Will you tell me the history of it?"

Beau's mother went on to tell Gracie that this quilt was made by her great-grandmother Sophie and her grandmother's circle of friends.

"I hear those quilting parties were something else!"

"I can definitely attest to that," GiGi chimed and toasted her iced tea glass.

Beau was incredibly surprised at the story too. "I haven't heard that story before."

"Yes, part of both of your heritage. The night Gracie stayed over, Joel and I were trying to think of something special to give you both. Joel remembered the quilt story, and we decided that would be the perfect gift. Here you go, sweet girl."

Gracie looked at GiGi, Aunt Ginny, and Uncle John, and they all nodded because they all remembered it, too.

"I always have the quilting racks ready to get started. Anyone interested?" GiGi asked.

* * *

When they arrived at Water's Edge, Beau couldn't wait to see Gracie's face when she saw the new pergola. Gracie was so excited and overwhelmed by what she saw. The little benches, flowers, butterflies, and pergola looked like something out of a garden magazine. Gracie was almost speechless and with eyes wide open said, "Wisteria!"

Never had she seen anything like this.

"How do you like our little paradise?" Beau asked.

"Looks like a beautiful place for a wedding,"

Liam said.

Beau leaned over to Liam and quietly said, "Are you trying to tell us something, man?"

Liam just smiled. "Hey, when are we taking the boat out again, Beau?" Liam inquired.

"Whenever you are ready! Beau answered. He swung around the pole and said, "I think we need to talk, right?"

"Right, but not now."

Beau nodded in agreement. "We'd better head back now. I know you two have to work tomorrow, so we won't keep you out too late, ha."

"Yes, we'd better head back now," Julie added.

Riding back to the Jackson residence, Julie said, "I almost forgot to give you something."

"What is it?" Gracie asked.

"We framed your sign from the car when you two escaped to your honeymoon. Here you go!"

Gracie took the sign that read, "And they lived happily ever after!"

"I love it! All right, where shall I place this?"

"How about inside the pergola?" Gracie queried.

"Perfect! Beau added with a big smile. "It's true, you know."

What's true?" Liam asked.

Beau pointed to the sign and smiled that killer smile.

* * *

"It sure was a fun day today. I guess we only have a few more days until we're back to work," Gracie said as she started slowly up the stairs.

"Yes, but let's focus on tonight and the rest of the week," Beau added, following her up the stairs. "Would you look at that moon tonight?"

"Not quite as bright as the Harvest Moon."

"We missed the Buck Moon, but the Corn Moon comes next," Beau added. We've got to spend more time enjoying the telescope that you bought me. After the Harvest Moon comes the Hunter's Moon, and it is supposed to be spectacular this year! Have you ever had a Mooncake?"

"No, Beau, but would be fun to make if we plan an Astronomy Night this fall! Do you think some of the bicycle group would want to come? It seems so long since we have seen them all. Maybe take the boat out, too?"

"I love the way you think. Let's do it!"

25

Gracie had woken up early to start work for the day and thought she would go downstairs to fix breakfast for Beau before he left for work. As she was walking down the stairs, she began to feel a little dizzy. She sat down on the stairs for a moment, then began feeling nauseous. As she sat there, she thought what she might have eaten that could have made her ill. Maybe the seafood, she thought.

She went about her business and decided to fixed Beau a healthy breakfast of oatmeal, fruit, and yogurt. She was afraid if she cooked, she might feel worse, smelling the scents of the meat and eggs. She opened the bay window to bring in the morning fresh air which seemed to help some.

Gracie could hear Beau getting ready for work. Seemed to be a quick shower though. As he quickly came down the stairs, he hollered, "Gracie, look at this!"

Gracie answered, "I am stirring your oats, so you'll have to come to me, Bodacious. What is it?"

"Mr. Sam Conway is asking if we would want to buy the Seaside Market. Wait, he is adding the Seaside Bookstore, too!"

"What in the world!" Gracie exclaimed.

"Gracie, he wants to sit down with us to talk about it later this week if we are interested."

"Seriously, this week?"

"Yes, what do you think?"

"Well, I know you know the business of the market, and I am familiar with the bookstore end of it from working with Uncle John. I guess it won't hurt to see what he has to say if that's something you are interested in."

"Yes, I am. I will set a time after work to meet with him. I can't wait."

Gracie wondered how this would all work in with Beau someday taking over his father's business and Gracie working more into her Uncle John's business. *"We'll leave this in God's hand to lead us. God's timing is everything,"* she thought.

Gracie leaned over toward Beau and said, "Now sit down here with me and give us a kiss."

"Us? Who is us? You have a little mouse or sea turtle in your pocket?"

"It's just a saying, you know."

"I know, but I had to tease you."

Gracie kissed Beau as he left for work and sat back down for another small cup of coffee on the porch. He waved all the way down the path to the road. How she loved that guy! As she sat there, she had a small wave of nausea again. "Ugh, no more coffee for me," she said aloud as she walked back inside and stretched out on the couch. *"I should probably lay here until this queasiness passes. Maybe a piece of toast will help,"* she thought.

* * *

Later that week, Sam Conway was eagerly

waiting at the market for Gracie and Beau to arrive. "What do you say we go over to the café to go over some numbers?" Sam asked.

"Sounds great," Beau responded.

After they gave their drink orders, Sam said, "Here is the bottom line."

Beau's eyes widened. "The numbers say it all, I guess."

Sam answered, "And numbers don't lie. Beau, you have worked for me for ten years and of all my employees, I felt that you were the one that really got it and understood the business. It's more than a job. It's about relationships and caring for the people that you serve."

"Well, thank you, Sam. You know I loved my job and appreciate all the years that you employed me!"

"It was my pleasure, Beau. Do you know that customers still come in and ask for you?"

"That says a lot, Beau," Gracie added.

"Yes, you never minded sweeping the floor, carrying groceries out to customer's cars, deliveries, stocking the shelves, or running the cash register."

"I might add that he makes a mean cup o' java too, but you already know that, Sam!"

"I sure do. Well think and pray on it and if your schedules allow, we can get together next week to finalize everything." Sam stood up and hugged Beau and Gracie and said, "I always felt like you were family, Beau, and now with Gracie here, it just all makes sense. I guess I'd better get back over there. Beau isn't there to fill in for me, ha!"

They all shook hands and left.

As they walked to the car, Gracie turned around and snapped a picture of Sam waving to them as he walked back into the market. "What a special man."

"Yes, I know," Beau agreed.

26

The whole gang was up for Astronomy Night at Water's Edge the following week and asked if this could be a monthly event. Beau and Gracie agreed as long as others would help to watch for the best nights of each month to stargaze. They all agreed to rotate it, which worked out greatly. Gracie and Beau volunteered to make mooncakes.

Liam said he would invite his co-worker, who has a minor in Astronomy and is hoping to go to work for NASA. He said that he could give us a lot of direction on when to plan our group get together around upcoming meteor showers, new moons, etcetera.

The food was great, and Beau outdid himself again with a lobster and seafood boil. The gang stayed close to the food and water. The sailboat, Souvenir, was ready for anyone who had their sea legs and was ready to take a short cruise. While some were out on the boat and riding scooters, Liam talked quietly to Beau. Gracie could see that something seemed important.

"Hey, I wonder what those two are up to?"

Julie replied, "Liam might be telling Beau that we are getting engaged this Christmas."

"What, girlfriend? Is it true?"

"Yes. Will you be my matron of honor?"

"Of course. I will. Are we telling this group

tonight?"

"For now, it's our secret. We haven't told our parents yet."

"Wow, I sure didn't expect to hear that tonight, and I am so happy for you two!"

Gracie hugged Julie and asked if she had any upcoming details and plans. They talked quietly about Julie's thoughts and Gracie listened intently.

"I guess it was a sign when you caught my bouquet, and Liam caught the garter!"

"I guess so. I am so happy Gracie. We have been going to church since the day we went to Church on the Beach with you and Beau. It was the part we were missing in our lives." Gracie hugged Julie.

Gracie pointed upward over the water. "It must be in the stars, Julie! Look, there's a shooting star!"

* * *

After Gracie and Beau cleaned up from the party, Beau twirled Gracie around and said, "I think the telescope was a hit!"

"Yes, I wonder how much money is in there after all of that."

"Yes, I forgot to tell them to bring their quarters."

"That's so funny, Beau."

"I had a couple rolls of quarters in the shed for them just in case they didn't have any change. Of course, they didn't!"

"Hey, I guess we are going to be in another wedding before too long."

Yes, and to think that we introduced them! I could see early on that they were getting along very well."

"And I could see that when Liam agreed to come to Church on the Beach, something had changed inside him for the better."

"Yes, Julie too. It's like their whole outlook on life and priorities had changed."

"Speaking of priorities, we need to sit down and talk about this acquisition together. I really want to know what you think, Gracie."

"Let's continue praying about it tonight and talk more tomorrow. I am suddenly so tired, and I'm not sure why."

27

Beau awoke early before Gracie and started to prepare breakfast. When Gracie smelled the bacon, she laid there a little longer. Am I going to be nauseous again? She wondered. She thought if she laid there for a few more minutes, she might feel better. After five more minutes, she arose and headed down the stairs to see Beau sitting quietly at the small table on the porch. He was watching two dolphins playing in the sea.

"There you and I are!" Beau chuckled.

"Yes, that is us out there, probably looking for the mermaids."

"Come and sit and I will get your breakfast for you."

"I think I will wait a little longer for breakfast. I'm a little nauseous again this morning."

"How about some toast and hot tea?"

"That would be good. If you don't mind."

"I'll be right back." Beau arose and went back inside to fix the tea and toast. "Fresh strawberry jam or apple butter," Beau hollered.

"Strawberry please!" Gracie didn't remember eating anything last night that would upset her stomach.

"Here you go. Be careful, the tea is steaming."

"Thank you. How is your workday looking? Will you be here in your home office or at the corp. office?"

"I'll be leaving shortly, and don't anticipate having a long day today. Thank goodness. I really believe God is leading us to buy the market and bookstore. Do you?"

"I do." Gracie answered.

"I'll contact Sam and let him know. I think he wanted to finalize all, so we can be the new owners as of January first."

"Yes, I believe that is what he said. I am pretty excited and happy about all of this, Beau. I forgot to tell you that Sam is going on the Maine trip with GiGi and company."

"Really? That's great! What do you say we go to the pier and ride the Ferris wheel tonight? It's been a while since we rode it together, Gracie."

"I would love that. You can put your arm around me, and we can snuggle really close, ha. Can we eat there, too? I have been craving a pronto pup!"

"For sure! That sounds great. I will text you when I'm on my way home. I'd better get going. I love you, Twinkle."

"I love you, Beau." She kissed him and he left for work, waving all the way down the lane to the main road.

Gracie thought she would start to feel better after eating her toast, but she just couldn't eat it right now, and began working. She was very productive for the first hour, then the wave of nausea started again. She laid down on the bed and wondered, *Could I be pregnant? We have only been married six months.* Gracie decided to drive to the drugstore to get a test to find out.

Gracie hurried in to take the test and the results were immediate. She sat down on the side of the tub in shock. There were two tests in the kit, so Gracie thought she should be sure and completed the other test. There were no doubts that she was pregnant. There wouldn't be any work completed the rest of the day now. Gracie had too much to think of and plan. She thought she would tell Beau at the top of the Ferris wheel tonight. It would make it very memorable for both of them. This was such an exciting time in their lives, and she wished she could tell her mom.

* * *

Beau texted Gracie around three o'clock to tell her he was on his way to pick her up. Gracie went outside to pull out the convertible and put the top down. She had put on her favorite outfit that Beau loved. As Beau pulled up, Gracie hollered, "Let's take Mama's car." Beau agreed and parked.

"Let me run in to change my clothes. I'll be right out."

Gracie went ahead and got into the car. She had placed the pregnancy test wrapped up in her purse to show Beau once they got to the top of the Ferris wheel.

"You are looking radiant today, Gracie. You must be feeling better?"

"Yes, feeling much better this afternoon," Gracie hinted.

* * *

As they were walking over to the Ferris Wheel, Beau recognized the ticket taker and asked that they get two rides, stopping on the top at the end of each ride for an extra five minutes. The person agreed, and Beau gave him an extra ten-dollar tip with two extra tickets.

"Did you do that the last time we rode?"

"Well, maybe, Beau smiled. Now come over here and give me a kiss." Beau put his arms around Gracie and squeezed her and gave her another quick kiss on the cheek.

As they rode around, Gracie waited until the last stop on top to show Beau the test.

Gracie was nervous and asked, "How do you feel about life changes?"

"Well, what do you mean? Buying those seaside businesses or inheriting our family's businesses?"

Gracie slid her hand in her bag and carefully unwrapped the test. "Neither. You're going to be a daddy."

"What? Say it again, Gracie!"

"You're going to be a daddy,"

"And you're going to be a mommy!"

At the same time, they yelled, "We're going to be parents!"

"So, there was a little mouse, actually two, in your pocket the other day when you asked me to give us a kiss."

"I didn't know it then, but God did."

It took a while for Gracie and Beau to fathom what God had blessed them with. They talked for hours as they walked the beach and planned how they would tell their family.

"It sure changes everything, doesn't it?" Gracie

asked.

"Yes, it does. It makes everything even better. I love you, Twinkle."

28

The next morning, Beau awoke and the first words that came out of his mouth were, "We've got to tell them, Gracie."

"Hello and good morning! What have you done with my husband? No, seriously, I know! How though? Group chat, Zoom meeting, or party?" Gracie teased.

"Definitely party! With Christmas a couple weeks away, it would be the perfect time."

"Agreed!"

"Maybe I'll throw a quiet Christmas Eve party here since it's my mom's birthday and invite our immediate family. What do you think?"

"I like the idea. I wish Julie and Liam could be here."

"I think Liam had told me all of their Christmas celebrations are on Christmas Day. I am sure Liam will be in the area. Can you check with Julie? I'll also get in touch with my parents and GiGi, Aunt Ginny, and Uncle John."

"You would do that for me?"

"Of course, I would."

"I'm afraid if I call, I might spill the beans!" Gracie laughed.

"Consider it done! I will make the calls right now."

***

Gracie went to the kitchen to start breakfast and the wave hit her again. She sat down while she mixed up the oatmeal for Beau. She thought she would stick to toast and tea for breakfast for herself for now. She hoped that this stage didn't last long.

Beau seemed to jump from the top of the stairs to the bottom by skipping too many steps. He danced into the kitchen and sang, "I'm going to be a daddy, and you are going to be a mommy." He pulled Gracie up and attempted to twirl her around. Gracie painfully tried to smile.

"I can see I need to wait until later in the day to twirl you, Gracie."

"Yes, maybe so. I do love it when you do it though, just not this early," she added.

"Everyone's in and Liam said that he and Julie would be here, so you don't need to contact her, scaredy cat."

"Thank you. I know I wouldn't be able to not tell her, and especially GiGi."

"Is there anything else that I can help with today?"

"I'll make out a grocery list for the party and maybe we can go to the Seaside Market next week to get our party supplies. What do you think Sam will say?"

"I forgot to tell you that he is going with GiGi and company on their trip to Maine."

"Maybe that's why he was wanting to wrap things up so quickly. It's hard to believe we will be business owners after the first of the year!"

"I am so excited! God has blessed us more than I had ever dreamed!"

"Amen to that!"

29

Everyone rolled in for the party on time. Gracie had all the Christmas decorations in place. She had set the Christmas tree under the stained-glass window, so the star in the window appeared to be the background for the star on the Christmas tree. Beau had lit the luminaries that his parents gave them from their wedding up the drive. Gracie placed the beef wellington and garlic mashed potatoes from the oven into the warming trays.

Table set, appetizers on the antique buffet, and drinks on the wet bar. Everyone else was bringing side dishes and desserts.

Beau came up behind Gracie and put his arms around her, embracing her baby bump. He patted the little bump, then got down on his knee to talk to Gracie's stomach. "This is going to be our first Christmas together and we are so blessed to share you with all of our family."

Gracie pulled Beau up to kiss him very sweetly, then he hugged her and kissed the top of her head. "What else can I do to help? I see the first car rolling in."

"I think we're ready! Are you ready with your good tidings of our great and greatest joy?" Beau shook his head yes.

* * *

Everyone came in very joyfully with their Dirty Santa gifts and laid them under the tree. Gracie could hear Uncle John saying, "Ho, ho, ho!" as he walked through the door with Aunt Ginny. Appetizers and drinks were served as guests arrived.

Beau announced that dinner was set at the antique oak table that had belonged to Gramma Sophie and asked everyone to gather around. As they sat down together, Beau said that he would like to read from the Bible because tonight was such a special night, not only was it when our Dear Lord was born but also it was his mother's birthday.

Beau began to read Luke 2:8-14 and was a little choked up, then said, "Gracie and I would like to bring you all some extra good tidings of our great joy." Everyone looked puzzled. "Well, Gracie and I recently found out that we are going to be parents of twin baby boys around the Fourth of July."

Everyone jumped back out of their seats and came over to Gracie and Beau. They spent most of the rest of the evening talking about the future and those two baby boys.

"Now, I want you all to know that I will be getting the quilting frames out soon for those of you who can join in!" GiGi exclaimed.

"That would be so fun," Callista added.

"We also wanted to share with you the names we have chosen for the babies," Beau said. "They will be named after Gracie's papa, who was GiGi's late husband and my father's dad, who is also no longer with us. They will be named Richie and Robbie, but we have not decided on middle names yet and are open to your suggestions!"

There were a few seconds of silence and a few tearful eyes, then a great shouting of "Congratulations!" "We can't wait," and so many other comments. You could see the excitement and hope of all that were there.

GiGi looked at Beau and rained her eyebrows. Beau winked at GiGi remembering the gift that Gracie's mother had left for her.

"Let's also sing happy birthday to Callista before we all forget it's her birthday with all this excitement!" GiGi said as she stood up and pulled out the chocolate sheet cake for Callista's birthday and lit her candles. We can have cake maybe after dinner and Dirty Santa, okay, Luv?"

"Perfect, GiGi!" Gracie answered. "Beau, would you ask the blessing?"

"Yes, Our Father...."

After the blessing, Beau said, "Dinner is served, please help yourselves!"

The joy in the air was thrilling, and everyone could not stop smiling. It was the best news for everyone!

Aunt Ginny asked, "Did you happen to use Gramma Sophie's recipe for the main course?"

"No, actually, it is my mother-in-law, Callista's recipe."

"It has been in our family for years and has always been a favorite around the holidays. I might add, it is Beau's favorite."

"Mine now, too!" Uncle John said.

"Mine, too!" Aunt Ginny added.

Julie and Liam held up their forks and said, "Ours, too!"

When dinner was over, everyone quickly headed to the front room to play Dirty Santa. It was quite competitive and was so much fun. Liam was the last to choose his gift and exclaimed that he was, of course, the winner. When he had completed his gift, he said, "Julie, come over here by me." He announced that not only was he the winner tonight, but that he and Julie had some incredibly special news to share with everyone. Liam announced that they were engaged earlier on this day. They had not set their date for the wedding. Now they definitely would have to work around another very special date to ensure that Gracie and Beau would be there.

Congratulations were flying around everywhere in the room and the mood was electrifying. "Well, since your parents are not in our company tonight and as your best man, I believe we need to make a toast! Grape juice for Gracie though!" Gracie nodded and was beginning to look a bit sleepy. Everyone raised their glasses.

"To high winds and mermaids, may you always be each other's northern star. Cheers!"

Uncle John added, "Time for a group selfie! Everyone on the stairs. We want to keep this night reminiscent as one of the best nights of this year. And may each year become brighter and more blessed."

"Cheers!" the group exclaimed.

"Beau is the tallest with the longest arms, so Beau, do you mind doing the honors?" Uncle John handed him his phone.

"Gladly, everyone in place. Gracie, please come over here right by me. Now everyone chime in together and say best blessings ever!"

"Best blessings ever!"

Acknowledgements and Thankfulness

I am thankful for the wisdom and loving support from my family, along with friends who are like family.

I am thankful for the First City Books group of authors – Molly, Nancy, Ben, Jim, and Travis who encouraged me to start writing again and to stay with it.

I am thankful for my editor, Gary Strohm, who has been a godsend.

Lastly, I am thankful that my Lord called out to me as a shepherd calling out to his sheep saying, "Come as you are." I am very humbled and blessed that He would use me in this way to share this message of love, hope, joy, and peace.

About The Author

T. L. Bishop is happy to announce her first novel, "Souvenirs". Terri lives with her husband in the Midwest and is an author, volunteer, and poet. She has a B.A. in Psychology and M.S. in Human Resource Development. She has used her life experiences to help coach and lead others in their daily work-life through Servant Leadership. Her hope is that readers will find "truth" in the pages of the story. She is open about her faith and is welcome to Christian public speaking for women's issues.

A portion of the proceeds of this book will benefit the homeless in the county in which she lives.

You can reach Terri at:
FaceBook.com/TLBishop2022

Made in the USA
Columbia, SC
14 March 2024